How to Fake
an Irish Wake

A MAGS AND BIDDY GENEALOGY MYSTERY BOOK ONE

ELIZA WATSON

HOW TO FAKE AN IRISH WAKE

Copyright © 2020 by Elizabeth Watson

All rights reserved by author.

Cover design by Lyndsey Lewellen at LLewellen Designs

ISBN-13: 978-1-950786-04-6 (paperback)

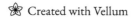 Created with Vellum

Books by Eliza Watson

NONFICTION

Genealogy Tips & Quips

FICTION

A Mags and Biddy Genealogy Mystery Series

How to Fake an Irish Wake (Book 1)

How to Snare a Dodgy Heir (Book 2)

How to Handle an Ancestry Scandal (Book 3)

How to Spot a Murder Plot (Book 4)

How to Trace a Cold Case (Book 5)

The Travel Mishaps of Caity Shaw Series

Flying by the Seat of My Knickers (Book 1)

Up the Seine Without a Paddle (Book 2)

My Christmas Goose Is Almost Cooked (Book 3)

My Wanderlust Bites the Dust (Book 4)

Live to Fly Another Day (Book 5)

When in Doubt Don't Chicken Out (Book 6)

FOR ADDITIONAL BOOKS VISIT

WWW.ELIZAWATSON.COM.

Dear Reader,

While growing up, I celebrated my Irish heritage on St. Patrick's Day by wearing green along with a pin that read, *The Luck of the Irish*. Yet the only family history we knew was that my mother's Flannerys had emigrated from Castlebar, County Mayo, and her Dalys from Kilbeggan, County Westmeath. In 2007, a twelve-day trip with my parents to Ireland turned out to be the most significant turning point in my life.

I can recall that breathtaking moment in the Kilbeggan cemetery, standing in front of an Irish rellie's grave for the first time. The same reaction most tourists have while standing on the Cliffs of Moher staring out at the Atlantic. Not only did Michael Daly's tombstone memorialize him and his wife but also two daughters. At that moment, I said, "Wouldn't it be great to return to Ireland and visit *living* relatives?" And so my genealogy research began.

Since that trip, I've researched more than twenty-five of my maternal and paternal Irish lines along with several Scottish ones. I've also assisted dozens of friends and family members with ancestry research in Austria, Canada, England, Germany, Hungary, and the US. Besides conducting online research, I have visited numerous historical archives, traipsed through hundreds of cemeteries (many now situated in sheep-filled fields), and located several family homesteads.

I never dreamed when I embarked on my adventure it would lead to me becoming a genealogist, meeting dozens of Irish rellies, writing two fiction book series set in Ireland, and buying a renovated 1887 schoolhouse in my Coffey ancestors' townland. Being able to combine my passion for writing and genealogy is a dream come true.

I hope you enjoy your trip to Ireland with Mags and Biddy. There's sure to be plenty of shenanigans!

Eliza Watson

To Mags Carter and Biddy Molloy
Here's to many more shenanigans.

Acknowledgments

Since first traveling to Ireland in 2007, my ancestors' homeland has not only become the inspiration for my second fiction series, but for most aspects of my life. Being unable to visit our Ireland home during this year's pandemic has reinforced my love for the country and its people. I miss everyone's hospitality, warmth, and wit, especially that of my dear friend and shenanigans partner, Mags Carter, and her best bud, Biddy Molloy. Thanks to both of you for all the laughs and for inspiring the super-sleuthing duo in my new mystery series. This book enabled me to spend time with all my Irish friends and family members in spirit. I treasure each one of you.

Thanks to Nikki Ford for your in-depth feedback, which was spot-on as usual. To beta readers Elizabeth Wright, Lisa Bean, Miriam O'Brien, Judy Watson, and Sandra Watson for all the wonderful input. To Dori Harrell for your fab editorial skills. To Chrissy Wolfe for your final proofreading tweaks. Thanks to you ladies, I can always publish a book with confidence. To Lyndsey Lewellen for another brilliant cover and capturing the spirit of Mags and Biddy.

One

"THERE'S WHISKEY IN THE JAR!" an elderly man sang out in the living room.

I eyed the empty liquor bottles in the kitchen's recycle bin, wanting to shout back, "Well, there's none in these *bottles*." But the musicians would figure that out on their next break when I served tea. Maybe they'd take that as a sign it was time to go home.

Out of respect for Grandma's love of traditional Irish music, I couldn't kick them out, despite being emotionally drained. And following her funeral, it'd been my idea that everyone came back to her house to eat leftovers from the two-day wake. Wanting a traditional wake—still the custom in much of rural Ireland—Grandma had lain in repose in her downstairs bedroom, in the bed I used to snuggle in with her when freaked out by the wind or rain whipping against my upstairs bedroom windows.

I didn't see myself ever sleeping in that bed again.

Eleven Christmas plum puddings lined the white counter

as if waiting for servers to light the brandy sauce on top and parade them through an elegant dining room rather than the small cottage. I'd paraded hundreds of flaming baked Alaskas through a cruise ship's dining room one summer while sailing from Vancouver to Anchorage. A rogue flame once singed my eyebrow, a sliver of which never grew back.

While growing up, I'd baked plum pudding with Grandma two Christmases in Ireland. It was tradition to make a wish while stirring the batter with a wooden spoon in a clockwise direction. My wish had been to spend every Christmas with Grandma. A wish that finally came true when I moved out of my parents' house in Chicago, old enough to choose where I spent the holiday.

My two older sisters had always chosen not to spend summers or holidays in Ireland. Precisely why they'd received only a few pieces of Grandma's jewelry—yet they'd expect me to share the sale of her house. Grandma had wanted me to use the money to travel the world and find myself. If Mom were alive, she'd have sided with my sisters, as usual.

I placed a plate on my raised palm and carried a plum pudding into the living room, just like in my cruising days. Grandma's elderly friend Edmond gave me a wink, looking dapper in a dark suit, sitting on a wooden chair playing a lively tune on the accordion. Two other men played a tin whistle and a fiddle. A group of spectators tapped their feet against the wood floor and sang along. Platters of food filled small tables, deep windowsills, and the bottom steps of the open spiral staircase.

I banged a fist against a cold radiator. Another bang and it hissed to life. I balanced the holiday dessert on top of the heating unit, then threw more peat on the fire in the green cast-iron stove tucked into a brick fireplace. Colorful twinkle lights and a lit-up ceramic tree decorated the wooden mantel. After Christmas, I always had the blues. Weeks of chaos preparing for the holiday and it was over in a flash, along with my stay in Ireland. Grandma having passed away two days before Christmas, I'd now be in a funk every December.

The French doors to the mudroom opened, letting in cold air and a tall, dark-haired guy, thirtyish—four years older than me—bundled up in a blue wool jacket and scarf. Empty-handed, he must not have received the memo that you never showed up at an Irish wake without food or drink. I let out a relieved sigh that he had. And actually, this was a *post*-wake.

I didn't recognize him from the wake or funeral. I'd certainly have remembered those bright-blue Irish eyes, seeing as I hadn't given a guy's eyes, butt, or smile a second glance since my fiancé had hopped a plane to New Zealand last year, breaking off our twenty-four-hour engagement. However, being ditched for a hundred exotic fern species was better than being ditched for *one* woman.

I went over and exchanged introductions with the man, who said his name was Finn O'Brien.

"Are you here for the wake?" I asked.

His broad shoulders went rigid, and his blue-eyed gaze darted around searching for the deceased. "Sorry. The door was open. I thought it was a holiday gathering."

"My grandma's funeral was today. This is a sort of after-party."

His panicked expression relaxed into a sympathetic one. "So sorry for your loss."

"Thanks. She was ninety. But she could have been a

hundred and it still wouldn't be easy. Would you like something to drink? Except whiskey. We're fresh out."

He shook his head. "I'm grand. I'll call in tomorrow if
that's okay?"

"Let's step outside," I yelled over a lively rendition of
"Finnegan's Wake," being sung as "Flanagan's Wake" in
honor of my grandma, Maggie Fitzsimmons née Flanagan.
Named after her, I went by Mags.

On my way through the mudroom, I tugged on a pair of
yellow wellies. They fit a bit snug with the wool socks and
purple leggings I'd thrown on after the funeral. I buttoned
up my green wool coat over my blue dress. I headed out the
door, and a cool breeze whipped my chestnut-colored hair
against my face. The earthy scent of peat puffing up from the
chimney wrapped me in a comforting embrace.

Finn smiled, eyeing my bizarre outfit. "Are you warm
enough?"

"I'm from Chicago. We're a sturdy stock." With the
setting sun, it finally felt warmer inside than out.

He glanced over at a sheep with pink splashes of dye on
its wool coat, dining on the front lawn. "Would you like me
to take him back in the field for ya?"

"He's not mine. Don't mind it grazing here. Will mean
less mowing." When I was eleven, an escaped sheep chased
me up the road to my childhood friend Biddy's family's pub.
I flew inside the bar without closing the door, and the sheep
raced in after me. If someone had videotaped the scene, it
would have gone viral. I wasn't about to confront this
animal. "If you aren't here for the wake, why are you?"

He slipped a black-and-white photo from his jacket

pocket—four young boys and a dog in front of Grandma's house, circa the early 1950s. I sucked at dating old photos. One glimpse at the attire and hairstyles and Grandma would have nailed the date within a month of when it was taken.

Finn smiled at the yellow house with a serene look. "My grandpa lived here. He's one of the boys in the snap. The other three were brothers or mates. I never knew him or my dad."

I gave him an apologetic look. "My grandma was the only owner of this house. She had a daughter, no sons. She lived here since the early eighties, when it was converted from an old schoolhouse into a home."

Finn's content look faded into one of disappointment. "He went to *school* here? I spent a week stalking mailmen and a load of quid buying rounds in pubs to locate this place."

I checked the photo's back for a date and found a phone number scrawled in pencil.

"That was my dad's contact number in Ireland. It's no longer in service. And try asking a front desk clerk for the name of a guest who stayed at their Liverpool hotel on January 8, 1990. They'll look at you like you're mad."

That wouldn't even have made my top-ten list for the craziest requests I'd gotten one winter while working the front desk at the Antlers Lodge in Montana. Like the rich elderly woman who demanded the stuffed moose and other wall mounts stop staring at her. Assigned with the task of addressing the paranoid guest's concern, I'd fetched a dozen pairs of sunglasses from the gift shop. I'd been told they're still sporting Foster Grants to this day.

"My mum and dad, both Irish, hooked up in a pub there.

The next morning when they parted ways, he gave her this snap with his number. Told her she'd need to ring him to return this priceless family photo."

"She decided not to call?"

"No, she did. She left two messages. One on voicemail, the other with a man. My dad never returned them. So she never returned the photo. I like to believe he had a good reason for brushing her off. I've invented a hundred different scenarios over the past thirty years. She moved to the States when I was eight. I threw a fit until she allowed me to stay here with my grandparents down in Wexford. I found this snap last year. My grandma filled me in on it. The fact that my mum kept the photo makes me think she held out hope of finding my father."

"I'm sorry. At least you know he went to school here."

"Along with hundreds of other kids."

"It was a small school. The rosters are on file at the Bally-caffey school, which is closed for the holiday. They're not online or at the Dublin archives." Where I'd spent much of my summers helping Grandma conduct genealogy research. "Actually, my grandma has an abbreviated copy of the rosters. She was a local historian and held an annual school reunion here. Once you get the photo dated, you could narrow down the school years and family surnames. The families are likely still in the area." I'd been putting off packing up Grandma's life's work and passion to donate to the local historical society. This would force me to sort through it. "I'll see what I can find. Stop by tomorrow."

Finn's frown curled into an appreciative smile. "That'd be grand, but don't want to be bothering ya after just losing your granny."

"No worries. My grandma would have wanted me to help you."

"I thought a paternal DNA test would help me. Had over two hundred matches with eleven different surnames. How can a paternal test have so many surnames? I thought there'd just be one. My father's."

"Not being a male, I can't take the paternal test. However, members in my online genealogy groups have had the same issue with numerous surnames. An advanced test would give you fewer, yet closer, matches with more conclusive results. The problem is some matches are connected to you from before surnames even existed, and surnames often changed over time due to adoptions, illegitimate children, all kinds of reasons. So the test might not even do you any good. Your father could biologically be a Gibbons but is living his life thinking he's a Grady because his four-times great-grandfather was adopted by a Grady couple. And some countries even based the surname on your father's occupation. You hope he wasn't a horse thief or murderer."

Finn smiled. "The closest match was a sixth-generation connection with the surname Burkhardt."

"Sounds German."

He nodded. "Seems the paternal test is a bit too costly for those merely curious whether they should be doing a German folk dance or an Irish jig. Few have taken it."

"DNA tests aren't as popular here as in the States. And it's a crapshoot if you'll even get a second or third cousin match. And many people use initials or a cryptic code for their profile name, preferring to remain anonymous. Most don't have family trees. If they do, the trees only go back to their grandparents or they're private, so you have to contact the matches to access them. Yet they don't respond to your message because they haven't signed into their account in a year."

Finn looked like I'd burst his DNA bubble. "Two weeks ago, I took a cheaper test for both paternal and maternal lines, which should provide much broader results with more matches. Will be getting the results in about a month. But what you said doesn't sound promising."

"Sorry. A lot of frustrated people have contacted my grandma for research assistance after DNA tests failed to help find their relatives." Including me. Last year I took a test on a whim and discovered my dad wasn't my biological father. We were both shocked by the news, especially since I'd been much closer to him than my mother. My mother passed away three years ago, taking the identity of my father to her grave.

"I'd be happy to take a shot of the picture and see if anyone can identify the boys. Neighbors will likely be paying their respects for days. Most of them attended school here."

"That'd be grand."

I slipped inside and returned with my cell phone and a Christmas pudding wrapped in foil. I presented the dessert to him. "Nobody leaves here empty-handed." One down and ten to go.

"My bed and breakfast doesn't have a fridge."

"No worries. It has the shelf life of a Twinkie."

Finn laughed, making me happy I'd lifted his spirits.

I snapped a shot of the photo.

He thanked me again and hopped into a sporty blue BMW. He drove down the narrow road, navigating around visitors' cars haphazardly parked along both sides.

I was sympathetic of Finn's quest to locate his father. I hoped I'd have better luck with his search than I'd had with mine.

Two

THE FOLLOWING AFTERNOON, I sat on the wooden floor upstairs in Grandma's lavender office. Sixty years of research and historical documents filled boxes, shelves, and cabinets. I'd found the rosters listing students who'd attended from 1876 until the school closed in 1975. As many as a hundred pupils were registered annually. Yet how many had attended on a regular basis when they were likely helping in the fields or at home? A hundred students would never have crammed into the small downstairs. The upstairs bath and two bedrooms had been a new addition when the schoolhouse was renovated into a residence.

For the past hour, I'd been paging through a large hardcover journal with handwritten stories from former students, who'd returned years later for a visit. At bedtime, Grandma would read me journal entries rather than fairy tales. I was catching up on stories added over the past ten years. Like an elderly man who reminisced about having let a ferret into the school. When it chased the teacher from the building, he'd bragged about having trained the animal to do so. Sadly,

Grandma had never thought to add her own stories to the journal. Even though I'd been carrying the tales around in my head for years, now that she was gone, I feared I'd forget them. I was far from a talented writer, but I needed to document her stories!

My heart raced.

I also needed to record family folklore and stories about our ancestors farming the surrounding land back five generations.

Only a second cousin still lived in the area, as well as two in Mayo. I wasn't sure about Grandpa Fitzsimmons's family, since none of them got along. But most of our Flanagans had immigrated to America or Australia, including my mother thirty years ago when she'd married my dad, Ryan Murray. A good Irish name, however, my dad was descended from the Murray Clan of Atholl in the Scottish Highlands. Their tartan was a lovely blue and green—very Irish looking, which was good since my DNA showed I wasn't the slightest bit Scottish.

I placed the journal on the antique student desk with my initials carved into the underside of the wooden top along with the initials MD, which had worn down over the years. Michael Daly, Matthew Doyle, Margaret Donnell... Years ago, I'd scoured Grandma's reunion rosters looking for the owner of the initials. Could have been one of hundreds.

I used to sit at the desk for hours, working alongside Grandma in her teacher's desk, both from the original schoolhouse. I'd once drawn a family tree in green crayon, each branch noting a family member. Grandma had praised my ability to trace our tree back to my two-time great-grandparents. Sadly, most people had difficulty naming family members beyond their grandparents.

The doorbell rang.

Finn O'Brien. I tightened the sash on my bulky velour robe as I trudged down the spiral staircase in my Berber slippers, the school roster in hand. I should have at least penciled in my missing sliver of eyebrow knowing I was having company, a hot Irish guy to boot. The only thing missing were hair rollers. I straightened my hair clip and tucked stray strands behind my ears. I'd seriously let myself go since Josh.

I answered the door to find two elderly ladies, rather than Finn, holding foil-covered aluminum pans. It would take me months to lose the weight I'd gained the past few days. The women had attended the funeral, but I didn't know their names.

"Thought you might be needing some comfort food." The lady in a red wool coat and matching hat presented me a pan that warmed my cold fingers.

If I couldn't eat all this food, maybe I could use the pans for bed warmers. The scent of potatoes and a red meat sauce filled my nose. Shepherd's pie. Hopefully, it was made with ground beef rather than the traditional ground lamb.

Lamb wasn't nearly as popular in the US as it was in Ireland, enabling me to have avoided it most of my life. When I was ten, my mother insisted I try it. The gamey taste had made me throw up. At that moment I announced I was a vegetarian. That diet lasted a week when I discovered that meant I also couldn't eat Chicken McNuggets or a Burger King Whopper. "Thank you. This is so sweet." I set the dish on a wooden chair, along with the other one that smelled of cheesy potatoes. "I appreciate it." Grandma would scold me for not inviting the women in for tea and biscuits, but I was talked out. I needed to get the office packed up before I left in three days for a B & B caretaker position in Maine. The owners spent the off-season in Florida. Hopefully, I didn't morph into Jack Nicholson from *The Shining* and go stark raving mad, isolated from civilization in a remote Victorian house with spotty internet and cell service.

The lady in red placed a sympathetic hand on my arm. "I'm sure you're exhausted, luv. We'll leave you be..." Yet her hand lingered, along with a concerned expression.

"Heard you're selling the place," the lady in green piped up in a disapproving tone.

How had they heard that? I'd just contacted a real estate agent this morning, and there was no *For Sale* sign in the yard.

I nodded.

The woman shook her head. "Had hoped it was merely a rumor. Can't imagine anyone but Maggie or *family* living here. Hope you'll at least be selling to someone in the area. Someone with an attachment to the schoolhouse. Someone who will appreciate and respect its historical significance. Someone..." Her cheeks reddened and her breathing quickened.

I feared she was on the verge of a heart attack. Her friend placed a calming hand on her arm.

"I promised my grandma the home would go to the perfect buyers," I assured her.

The woman's scowl relaxed slightly. "Suppose that's something anyway."

The lady in red nodded in agreement.

They wished me luck. In life or finding a homeowner

they approved of, I wasn't sure. They got in their small gray car and motored down the road.

Grandma hadn't expected me to keep the house, knowing I could never afford the monthly bills let alone make all the needed repairs. I'd never even *rented* an apartment. I used my dad's address for mail and crashed at his Florida condo when I was between seasonal jobs. At twenty-six, the thought of being a responsible homeowner was overwhelming. And a house was meant to be lived in, especially in Ireland, to keep out the dampness and prevent mold. But I'd promised Grandma I'd find the perfect owners. And now I'd promised those two women the same.

With no space in the kitchen's small refrigerator, I stuck the dishes in the shed on a shelf between a pan of lasagna and old paint cans. I had to find a homeless shelter or church that would accept a food donation.

I decided to walk up to McCarthy's pub to see if some older locals enjoying a pint could identify the boys in Finn's picture. And Biddy should be off work. She'd been the first person I'd called when I'd discovered my dad wasn't my biological one. She'd helped me through my twenty-four-hour failed engagement. And I wouldn't have survived the two-day wake without her. A pro at emptying the pub at closing time, Biddy had kicked visitors out at midnight, enabling us to take a nap before visitation resumed at 7:00 a.m.

I slapped a note on the door, informing Finn of my location. It seemed odd that he hadn't stopped by, anxious to see if I'd found the rosters with clues to his father's identity.

I walked a quarter mile up the narrow, pothole-filled road to the small white pub. A gold-lettered sign reading

McCarthy's hung over the blue door. Inside, a crowd of younger guys were shouting at two horses on TV sprinting neck and neck toward the finish line. A loud cheer erupted. Everyone raised their pints in celebration.

Biddy's dad rang a bell behind the bar. He pushed up the sleeves of his blue plaid button-up shirt, preparing to replenish drinks. Spotting me, he walked out from behind the bar and gave me a hug. "How ya doing, Maggie Mae?"

Daniel McCarthy had given me that nickname years ago, and it'd stuck.

Still in his comforting embrace, I nodded my head against his chest. He was almost a foot taller than my five foot three inches. "Hanging in there."

He stood back, concern dimming his blue eyes. "Look like ya could be using a pint."

"Sure. I don't have far to walk home."

"Wanna bet on the ponies?"

I shook my head. "Not feeling too lucky right now."

I sat on a lone stool around the side of the bar while he called in bets. A large framed photo of a sheep hung on the wall over the register. The animal's back hooves on the floor, front ones on the bar, it was sniffing a pint of Guinness next to the toes of my pink tennies. I'd have won a gold medal for the high jump, springing from the floor up onto the bar without any assistance. Someone had snapped a pic of that infamous day I was chased by a sheep.

I was a bit of a legend at McCarthy's pub.

Biddy breezed through the door behind the bar, leading from their residence. Having just come from work at a hospital's pediatric ward, she had on a green-and-red nurse's uniform with Snoopy dressed as Santa, Woodstock an elf.

Her dark-blond hair was pulled back in a lopsided ponytail—a low-maintenance style considering her mom, Ita, was a hairdresser.

The last adventurous thing Biddy had done with her hair was when we were twelve. We had the hots for fourteen-year-old twins Niall and Noah Doyle. Wanting to look more mature, we raided her mom's hair-color stash. My overprocessed light-brown tresses turned out darker than Morticia Adams's. Going for a light-auburn shade, Biddy had ended up with Bozo orange. Our punishment was living with the new hair color until it grew out. We'd hidden our embarrassing hair under Biddy's blond ringlet wigs she wore at step dancing performances. Rather than looking older, we'd resembled a Shirley Temple tribute duet. Impossible to pull off the curly wigs without the fancy dance dresses, we'd spent the rest of the summer avoiding the Doyle boys.

Biddy kissed her dad on the cheek as he set a bottle of hard cider and salt-and-vinegar-flavored potato chips on the bar in front of me. My usual. "Dinner will be late. Was a car accident when I was getting ready to leave work, and they were down a nurse, so I stepped in to assist."

"How bad?" he asked.

"Bloody awful." She grimaced. "Can't believe I just said *bloody* about a car accident. No wonder I didn't get promoted to supervisor. He's critical. A gorgeous fella. Good thing he was driving a BMW rather than a Peugeot or he'd have been toast."

Gorgeous fella? BMW? The hairs on the back of my neck stood at attention. It seemed strange that Finn hadn't yet shown up.

"Is he about thirty, tall, dark hair, a five-o'clock shadow?"

Biddy nodded, quirking a curious brow. "Been working on your psychic abilities, have ya?"

The hairs on my arms joined the ones on my neck. "Do you know his name?"

"Finn O'Brien."

My jaw and bag of crisps dropped onto the wooden bar.

Three

I'D FILLED Biddy in on my brief genealogy-bonding encounter with Finn O'Brien. The following morning, she met me at the hospital's entrance and escorted me past the nurses' desk so I wouldn't have to explain my relationship, or rather lack of one, with the patient. She then scurried back to the pediatric ward.

I was walking into Finn's room when a middle-aged blond woman rushing out nearly ran me over. Rather than apologizing, she flew down the hall. How rude. And who was she if only relatives were allowed to visit? Biddy hadn't mentioned any family having been notified. I'd have to ask her if Finn's grandparents in Wexford had been contacted, if they were even still alive, and his mother in the States.

I walked past the white curtain drawn around the bed and sucked in a startled gasp at all the tubes and beeping machines connected to Finn. His gauze-wrapped head lay against a white pillow. The bluish-purple bruises on his face and puffy eyelids looked like a bad Monet painting. He'd come to the Midlands to meet his father, not his death.

Feeling faint, I braced a hand on the bed's side rail. I'd have to be a much more cautious driver, now responsible for getting myself around without Grandma. Finn had been raised driving on the opposite side of these narrow roads and encountering obstacles like sheep and tractors around every bend. Yet look at what had happened to him.

I took an encouraging breath and forced a smile. "I found the school rosters." My tone was perky and optimistic, in case he could hear me. "Once we identify the four boys, we can check their names against the student lists and find your father." Easy peasy. "My shot of your picture could be better. Would you mind if I take another one?" I paused, as if waiting for his answer, before I started snooping.

I found his blue wool jacket hanging in the closet, his brown shoes on a shelf. I was surprised neither had been trashed in the accident. The photo wasn't in the jacket pocket where he'd slipped it from to show me. I'd have to have Biddy check his wallet and personal belongings.

I returned to the patient as his swollen eyelids struggled to open. Pain meds and exhaustion had dulled his bright-blue eyes.

I smiled. "Hi, remember me?"

He squinted at me through slitted lids, then nodded faintly.

"I'm going to get a nurse."

He reached out a hand, dropping it shy of my arm.

I placed my hand on his. "It's okay."

"No, I…" His voice cracked, his throat too dry to speak. "…need…you…"

"Need me what?"

"Be careful." His gaze darkened. "Not safe."

Goose bumps raced across my skin.

His eyelids closed.

"No, wait." I gave his hand a gentle squeeze. "Why am I not safe?"

He slipped back into unconsciousness.

Panic rippled through my body; my breathing quickened.

Why would he warn me to be careful? Had he heard me talking about showing the photo around? Had Finn been showing people the photo prior to his accident—and it hadn't been an *accident*?

Maybe someone in a pub had recognized the boys in the photo and Finn had disclosed his relationship to one of them. If I flashed the photo around trying to identify the boys, would that person try to stop *me*?

I promised Finn I'd be careful and return tomorrow for a visit. The poor guy didn't have any family in the area. Except maybe for the woman who'd slammed into me.

I went out to the nurses' station, decorated with red garland and small bowls filled with green and red foil-covered candy. A slender middle-aged woman smiled at my red sweatshirt. *Beer, Brats, and Jell-O Shots.* I'd bought it the summer I'd cleaned vacation cottages in northern Wisconsin. Thanks to my second-worst job, I learned the art of slurping liquor-spiked gelatin from a shot glass.

"Ah, that's great craic, isn't it now?" she said.

I told her about Finn briefly coming to. Having bonded over my sweatshirt, I felt safe asking a few questions. "I met a visitor leaving his room but didn't catch her name."

"A visitor, ya say? Nobody checked in with me."

Why wouldn't a relative of Finn's have inquired on his

condition? Asked to speak to his doctor? A family member or friend wouldn't need to skulk around the corridors waiting for an opportune moment to sneak into his room.

"And I'm so sorry about your fiancé," the nurse said.

I couldn't believe Biddy had blabbed to this woman that I'd been dumped for some stupid exotic ferns in New Zealand.

The nurse peered over at Finn's room. "His vitals have stabilized. A very good sign. He'll be grand."

Finn was supposedly my fiancé? That was how Biddy had scored me visitation rights?

I peered down at my tan shoes, nibbling on my lower lip, trying to hide my surprised look while I scrambled for a response. If I set this woman straight, Biddy could get in deep trouble. I let out a depressed sigh and morphed into a grieving fiancée. "Thank you. It's been a difficult time." Genuine tears welled up over having just lost Grandma and now Finn confiding in me about his accident, which likely wasn't an *accident.*

The kind nurse handed me a tissue and several pieces of foil-covered chocolate.

An opportune time to play the sympathy card, I asked, "Do you think I might be able to see his belongings? There's a photo in his wallet I'd like to have." I unwrapped a piece of milk chocolate and popped it into my mouth, letting the creamy richness melt against my tongue.

"Of course, luv." The nurse left and returned moments later with a black leather wallet.

I opened it with shaky hands and slipped out the plastic picture holder containing several *colored* photos. No black-and-white one of young boys in front of Grandma's tucked between the plastic sleeves. No way would Finn have entrusted anyone with the only clue to his father's identity. And it was too important to have misplaced. But who'd have stolen an old family photo from his hospital room?

That blond woman.

It would seem suspicious if I didn't take a picture, so I slipped one of Finn and a brunette woman from the plastic. I thanked the nurse and gave her the wallet and my cell number in case there was any change in Finn's condition. I pocketed several more chocolates for the road. She wasn't going to judge my candy hoarding in my fragile emotional state.

As I neared Grandma's small blue car in the back lot, someone approached from behind. My gaze darted over my shoulder at dry leaves rustling against the pavement. I let out a relieved sigh. What was with my sudden paranoia?

Actually, I'd inherited the condition from my mother, although not as severe. If an exterminator knocked at the door offering a discount, she'd be outside searching the perimeter of the house for the army of ants the man had released, sabotaging our house. When she once turned down a window salesman, she told him, "I supposed now I'm going to wake up tomorrow and find a baseball thrown through my living room window." The salesmen in our neighborhood never had a chance. Whereas if a lawn service knocked on Grandma's door, she'd look at it as brilliant timing, because she was tired of mowing the grass every other day. If the service was discounted, she'd feel so blessed she'd be out buying lotto tickets.

However, my paranoia might not be unfounded since

someone had likely stolen Finn's only clue to finding his biological father and had run him off the road.

Stop it! I didn't know for sure that was what he was referring to. Why would someone want to hurt Finn over a seventy-year-old photo of four young boys? Maybe the photo was still in his car. I needed to search his Bimmer. And I needed to advise the police about Finn's warning.

I bolted to Grandma's car and locked myself inside. My phone rang in my purse, about catapulting me through the roof. Shane Reilly. My real estate agent. He wanted to show Grandma's house to an interested couple that afternoon. I twisted my mouth around, debating telling him I was busy. Yet if I didn't show the house, I couldn't sell it. Despite an overwhelming sense of sadness, I agreed.

First, I had to stop by the garda station.

I explained to the older female police officer behind the desk that Finn told me he'd been run off the road.

She gave me a blank stare, her green eyes reflecting zero interest. "That's it? He said, 'You need to be careful'?"

Repeating Finn's warning didn't sound nearly as foreboding as when he'd said it. Yet I didn't care for her condescending tone. "He also said 'not safe.' He sounded afraid and had a scared look in his eyes."

"He was likely telling ya to drive carefully on the roads in this area. They can be quite dangerous."

I reined in my frustration. "That's not it. I think someone ran him off the road or did something to cause his accident."

"There was no evidence of another vehicle being involved. However, the car was wrecked. An eyewitness told the person who rang 999 that the fella took the corner too fast."

"Wait a sec. The eyewitness didn't call 999?"

She shook her head. "Didn't have a phone on 'em."

"Who doesn't carry a cell phone nowadays? My ninety-year-old grandma had one."

She glared at me. "Maybe it wasn't charged."

"Was the witness a man or a woman?"

"Not at liberty to say."

Fine. "Can I see Finn O'Brien's car?"

"As I said, it was wrecked."

"I left a photo in it."

"The car was checked thoroughly. No snap." The officer's tone was dismissive, yet her gaze was curious. Why was I worried about some photo while my friend was fighting for his life? "What did you say your name is?"

"Ah, Mags Murray."

"You're American?"

"I live in the US, but I have dual citizenship."

Technically, I hadn't *lived* anywhere since I'd landed my first temp gig at age nineteen, harvesting cranberries in Oregon. Living on free cranberry products that fall had provided me with a lifetime tolerance to bladder infections, yet a low tolerance for the bitter-tasting berry.

The officer began documenting my answers in the computer. "And how exactly did you know Mr. O'Brien?"

My breathing quickened. Should I continue with Biddy's fiancée story? Lying to the police was a bad idea, yet if they spoke to the hospital and the nurse mentioned I was Finn's fiancée...

The officer tapped an impatient finger against the keyboard.

"A close friend," I said.

"What exactly was this a snap of?"

I showed the woman the photo on my phone and explained Finn's interest in the four boys. "What if he was run off the road because of this picture?"

"Someone tried to kill him over a family snap?"

"Maybe the person doesn't want a skeleton in his closet destroying his family. I don't know."

Unless an actual skull and bones were found in someone's closet, this officer wouldn't be investigating it. I thanked her—for what I had no clue—and left.

Had Finn's blond visitor been the eyewitness? Wanting to see if her attempt on Finn's life had been successful? And to steal his photo? Who was she, and why wouldn't she want Finn to find his biological father? If she were local, she'd have been taking a risk showing up at the hospital when someone might have recognized her and questioned her interest in Finn. However, desperate people often made mistakes. If that was the case, maybe she made another one. One that didn't put Finn's life in further danger.

Yet maybe the person had followed Finn up here from Wexford and the accident was unrelated to the photo. A psycho ex-girlfriend seeking revenge. The woman at the hospital was at least twenty years older than Finn and a bit frumpy compared to the goddess I pictured him dating. Either way, if the blonde had showed up at the hospital to see if her job was done, she knew it wasn't.

She might decide to finish it.

"What a perfect spot for a cement patio." The young woman in a black suit gestured to Grandma's cobblestone walk in back, bordered with green buds that would soon be blossoming into yellow daffodils. The path led to a wooden trellis wrapped in rosebush branches anxious for spring. Every summer, I'd helped Grandma lovingly tend to her flowers. A curious farmer in the adjoining field peered over at us from his tractor crawling along. I gave him a wave. He waved back, continuing to stare.

"That old wall won't be lasting long," the husband said. "Might as well tear it down and replace it with brick."

Tear down what was left of the schoolhouse's original wall that Grandma had repaired each time a stone became loose?

My breathing quickened, and an annoying buzzing filled my ears, blocking out the rest of the couple's devastating plans. "I'll be inside."

I bolted through the conservatory, past two pails on the tile floor, waiting to catch rainwater. I'd removed the mousetraps before the showing but had forgotten about the buckets. I flew into the kitchen, my yellow wellies leaving a trail of wet tracks on the wood floor. I flipped the switch on the electric kettle, and steam soon rose into the air. Gulping down the hot golden tea, I went into the living room, where the fire had already died out in the green cast-iron stove. I'd be voted off that show *Survivor* in five minutes flat.

I banged a fist against the temperamental radiator, and it

hissed at me. I went over and brushed a gentle finger over the ceramic Christmas tree on the mantel, and my shoulders relaxed. The tree had occupied that same spot every holiday for as long as I could remember. At age twelve, I spent my first Christmas with Grandma. When I'd whined about not having a real tree, we'd decorated the rose trellis out back with twinkle lights, visible from the living room window.

And so began another holiday tradition.

The enthusiastic couple breezed into the house as if they already owned the place. My back tensed.

"The fireplace must go," the woman said to her husband. "The wretched yokes are filthy."

When renovating the schoolhouse into a three-bedroom home, the master craftsman had maintained the integrity of the original fireplace, leaving several old stones exposed among the new brick.

"Then you'll have to replace most of the radiators," I said. "And the fuel tank. All the fuel on this road was stolen two years ago. The thief drilled a hole near the bottom of the tank, so now it only holds a hundred liters despite being plugged. And the boiler hasn't been serviced for years since my grandma rarely used fuel."

The agent shot me a cautioning glance to not discourage the potential buyers. "It's only twenty minutes from the motorway," he reminded them for the dozenth time.

Grandma would have preferred someone with ties to the schoolhouse and community rather than a Dublin couple. Everyone in the townland over the age of fifty had gone to school here and looked after the house as if it were their own.

The woman peered around, smiling. "Will be grand for Felix and Fiona."

"Your children?" I asked. "Are they twins?" Grandma would love the thought of a family living in her house.

"Our tarantulas," the man said.

I bit down on my lower lip, stifling a horrified squeal.

The woman tapped a finger against her red lips. "I'm thinking shades of dark gray for all the yellow walls."

"I'll be in touch." I ushered them toward the front door.

"But we'd like to make an offer," the woman said over her shoulder.

"That's nice." I practically shoved them out the door, along with the agent, who was wearing a baffled look.

"Ten thousand over asking price," the husband shouted at the slamming door.

No way were they turning Grandma's house into a goth home for tarantulas. Not even for fifty thousand over asking price. The place had only been on the market for two days. I figured I'd be on the other side of the world, emotionally and physically distanced from the sale.

No peat to make a fire, I headed out the back door with a Tesco grocery bag. I traipsed across the tall grass to the wood-shed. A half dozen cows moseyed over to the wire fence and watched me struggle with the shed's rusted padlock.

It began raining. Not a drop of warning—just straight to a full-blown downpour. I loosened the strap on my robe and managed to karate kick the padlock, jarring the clasp open, denting the metal shed. I flew inside the structure. A mouse scampered under the pile of peat, startling me. Lying to myself that he was more scared of me than I was of him, I quickly loaded the bag with peat. I slipped the lock back into place without securing it, allowing me easier access next time. I gave the nosy cows a wave and raced back to the house.

A steady stream of rain was filling the buckets on the conservatory's tile floor. I replaced the buckets with the kitchen and bathroom garbage cans. I stripped off my drenched sweatshirt. The dryer was in the boiler shed, so I draped it over the couch arm next to the fireplace. I threw on a blue sweatshirt that read *Marry Me, Sail for Free*. From the summer I worked banquets on the Alaskan cruise ship. At the end of the season, employees had received a free future cruise. Having taken me months to get my equilibrium back in check, I never took the trip. And now I only wore the sweatshirt in private after receiving several lewd marriage proposals.

I set a cup of tea on the living room cocktail table displaying dozens of postcards under a glass top. Places I'd visited while working temp jobs, including a West Palm Beach resort. I'd worked there one winter as a dog walker and sitter for the rich and famous. The best job ever, except for having to arrest misbehaving pets during the night and take them to doggie jail—a private doghouse with a four-poster bed where they dined on gourmet treats. Pet owners had tested my work ethic, trying to slip me a hundred bucks to ignore the other guests' complaints. I was proud to say I'd never accepted a bribe.

I plopped down on the overstuffed, comfy red couch with my laptop and pulled up Ancestry.com. I had thousands of fifth-to-eighth cousin DNA matches. Too distant to know if they were paternal or maternal relations. Five third-to-fourth cousin matches, likely maternal. And zero first- or second-cousin ones. The only thing the test had confirmed was that instead of being half-Scottish like I'd thought, I was English and French. I despised kidney pie and escargot.

Enjoying a good Bordeaux didn't lessen the blow that, in a matter of seconds, my DNA test results had robbed me of my Scottish identity. Suddenly years of Dad and me attending the Scottish Highlands Games and Red Hot Chili Pipers concerts no longer held quite the same meaning. Thankfully, Dad had no interest in genealogy. I'd have been devastated to learn I wasn't a blood relation to the generations of Murrays in my family tree. Not that my discovery had made me love Dad any less.

I just somehow felt...adrift.

I clicked out of my account and perused social media sites for Finn O'Brien. I knew nothing about the handsome man from Wexford except that he was searching for his biological father. And that someone possibly wanted him dead.

After cruising the internet, the only thing I learned was that Finn was a private person with zero social media presence. No post of him holding a sign with his birth date and location, seeking Facebook users' assistance in locating his biological father. I finally found him on a website for a woolen goods factory with five store locations in Ireland. I'd bought some gorgeous scarves at their Dublin shop. He managed the business, family owned and operated for four generations. Obviously on his mother's side.

The doorbell rang.

I let Biddy in.

She shrugged off her favorite green fleece rugby jacket over her nurse's uniform with pink flying unicorns. Despite it being a national sin, Biddy hated the sport but loved the jacket. "I need a drink." She straightened her lopsided ponytail. "Work is brutal right now. People back for the hollies forget how damp Ireland is and can no longer tolerate the weather. And my manager is in a foul mood, insisting all the staff goes back to wearing the boring blue uniforms because that's what she has to wear. I spent a load of quid on my new uniforms and threw away my old ones. I won't be buying another."

Biddy made a beeline for the kitchen. The cork popped on a wine bottle, and she returned with two glasses of red. She set them on the cocktail table, then plopped down on the couch's matching loveseat. She eyed my laptop next to her glass. "Shopping for more woolies, are ya?"

I admitted to having been researching Finn and filled her in on his warning, the blond mystery woman, and the surly garda officer.

Her blue eyes widened. "Someone might be trying to kill the poor bloke?"

"Can you imagine someone trying to murder my *fiancé*?"

Biddy wore a guilty grin. "I had to tell her something."

"Well, you should have told *me*. Why would someone want to kill him over trying to find his biological father?"

"Sex, greed, revenge, hate, love..."

"How could it be any of those reasons when the person can't even know Finn?"

"An illegitimate child could cause a wee bit of family drama."

"It could also be a psycho ex-girlfriend who followed him up here from Wexford, thinking he was hooking up with some woman."

"Hope she didn't follow him here that day and now she's after you."

"Thanks. That makes me feel safe, especially after Finn told me to be careful. Let's hope he's safe in the hospital."

"He's grand."

"What type of person isn't on social media?"

"A private one." Biddy waggled her fingers in a mysterious manner. "Like one in the witness protection program."

"I doubt that's the case, since he's not hiding his identity, openly searching for his biological father."

"How do we know that's his real identity? Maybe the whole father thing is a lie and he's searching for the criminal responsible for him going into hiding."

"He's not in witness protection when he's on his company's website. Just wish I could learn more about him."

"Have a bit of a crush on the fella, do ya?"

I shook my head, yet heat flushed my cheeks.

It was the wine.

"Did a bit of investigating myself," Biddy said. "Talked to my friend Nellie, the nurse minding Finn. His granny is too frail to make the trip up from Wexford, and his grandpa passed away. They haven't been able to reach his mum in the States." She took a gulp of wine. "So did the Dublin couple make an offer on the house?"

My gaze narrowed. "How'd you know I had a showing? And that the couple was from Dublin?"

"The entire townland knows you had a showing and their gray Volvo had a Dublin plate."

"That farmer could read the car's plate?"

"No clue. But Marjorie Walsh could. After walking her dog, Mia, past, she stopped in at her friend Bev's, whose husband was on his way to our pub..."

"Okay, I get it. They offered ten thousand more than the asking price."

Biddy's lips pursed with disapproval. "Sold out for a measly ten thousand over asking price, did ya?

"Not yet." I told her about the hideous changes they planned to make.

"Anyone buying the house is going to want to make changes to fit their own style. Are ya sure that's the reason you didn't accept the offer?"

"It is."

Biddy rolled her eyes. "Whatever."

Grandma and her house had been the only stabilizing forces in my life. Yet how could I financially afford or justify keeping the place now that Grandma was gone, when I'd chosen not to live here when she was alive?

Four

THE NEXT MORNING the same nurse at the hospital's reception desk confirmed that Finn's female visitor hadn't returned. "He must have come to for a bit," she said. "He wrote this on the pad of paper from his bedside locker. It was resting on his chest." She handed me a sheet of paper with *Be Careful... Little Red Riding Hood* scrawled in shaky hand-writing.

The fairy tale?

I arched a curious brow, snatching a piece of foil-covered chocolate from the bowl. "What does it mean?"

"That the little girl shouldn't have believed the wolf was her granny?"

I shrugged, unwrapping the candy and popping it into my mouth.

Entering Finn's room, I plastered on a perky smile despite the fact that he looked worse than the previous day. His bluish-purple bruises were now chartreuse colored and looked even more painful. I hesitated to fill him in on my visit to the garda station, not wanting to upset him if he didn't recall his accident and warning me to be careful.

"I'm going to visit my grandma's friend. A local historian, he'll be able to date the photo and possibly identify the boys." I glanced down at the sheet of paper. "What did you mean by Little Red Riding Hood?"

Did that fairy tale have something to do with Finn's accident?

"Little Red Riding Hood..." After repeating the title a dozen times, an idea popped into my head.

What if it'd been a *little red* car *hood riding* his bumper?

Maybe Finn's brain was using word association to recall the accident. Or maybe it'd been his favorite childhood fairy tale and he was delusional.

Either way he needed to remain in the safety of his hospital bed. Yet just how safe was it if some strange blond woman might have run him off the road, then swiped a photo from his jacket pocket while he was lying in bed unconscious? Good thing I had a photo of the picture.

Or was it?

If someone knew I had it, they might come after *me*. I didn't have doctors, nurses, or hospital security to protect me.

Merely Biddy.

I was standing in front of the same garda officer I'd pleaded my case to yesterday. Her negative and judgmental attitude hadn't improved.

Her green-eyed gaze narrowed on me. "That's it? Little Red Riding Hood?"

"And be careful. Don't you see? *Red* was the color of the *little* car, and he saw the *hood* coming at him. That's all that stuck in his mind. What color was the eyewitness's car, who left without calling 999?"

"I'm not at liberty to say." Yet she looked mildly intrigued for the first time.

"It was red, wasn't it?"

"The poor fella had just woken up after a near-fatal car crash. I'm sure he was afraid and a bit disoriented."

"Can you at least document this so it's on file?"

"No worries."

No worries she'd do it or she wouldn't?

"When the hospital notifies us that he's awake and in condition to give a statement, we'll visit him."

"What if he's never in condition to give one?" What if he never regained consciousness? My chest tightened.

The officer wasn't taking my Little Red Riding Hood theory seriously. Finn didn't have anyone but me to help him. *How* I was going to help, I hadn't a clue. But I had to try. I wasn't a police detective, but I'd helped Grandma solve plenty of genealogy mysteries. The attempt on Finn's life proved he was close to finding his father. And more so than a police investigation, maybe he needed a genealogist to not only find his father but to solve who'd run him off the road. Me solving the case would certainly irk Officer Negative Nancy.

I hadn't told my future employer about Grandma's death, having assumed I'd have everything settled in Ireland prior to starting work. I called the B & B owner, who was sympathetic for my loss and understanding about me needing to start a week later. That gave me seven days to find Finn's father and the person who'd attempted to kill him.

For Finn's sake, I hoped the two didn't turn out to be the same person.

Twenty minutes later I was on the road to Drumcara, retracing Finn's route before the accident. A huge black circle on a yellow road sign had me easing up on the gas pedal. In Ireland, a squiggly line cautioned twisty corners ahead, which the locals maneuvered like NASCAR drivers. A right-angle warned of a sharp bend. But a large black circle was the equivalent of Deadman's Curve—which had ended James Dean's life on that fatal California day.

Luckily, the bend hadn't been deadly for Finn.

Skid marks scarred the blacktop, and tires had dug ruts in the narrow shoulder where glass debris sparkled in the sunlight. Several damaged hedges revealed a stone fence behind, which had stopped Finn's car. I slowed to a crawl, glancing in the rearview mirror at the silver car riding my bumper. A red car hood might have been the last thing Finn had seen before being run off the road.

Goose bumps slithered up my back.

There wasn't room to pull off, which was fine. No need to stop and be nosy. I didn't hope to discover any clues at the scene of the crime unless Finn's photo had flown out a shattered car window. It was *prior* to the accident that interested me.

If Finn had been flashing the picture around Drumcara

and knocked on the wrong door, or rather the *right* door, maybe he'd found his father or his family without having known it. Maybe they hadn't been keen on being found. Had Finn been honest about his interest in identifying the young boys?

A white sign greeted me at Drumcara's village limits—the town's name in both English and Gaelic. I popped into a convenience store for a latte. Ireland's quick stops had the best coffee machines. When I breezed through the door, I stifled a surprised gasp. I couldn't believe my luck. Good luck. There behind the counter stood the blond middle-aged woman who'd slammed into me when fleeing Finn's hospital room. Chatting with a customer, she gave me a friendly smile, no glint of recognition in her eyes. Her gaze also wasn't darting around, frantically searching for an escape route.

Heart thumping against my chest, I dispensed a steaming latte into a paper cup and headed to the counter as the customer left. I gave the woman a friendly hello and a curious smile. "You look familiar. Were you at the hospital in Navan yesterday?"

She nodded. "I was."

"Visiting Finn O'Brien, right?"

Her smile faded into a somber expression, which made her look even older than her heavily tanned skin. "That poor lad. Such a shame." Her voice cracked from a two-pack-a-day habit rather than emotion. "I hope he's doing better."

I frowned. "No change." Except he'd woken up long enough to tell me he'd been run off the road by a little red car. No car sat in the store's parking lot. I opted not to provide the promising news in case the woman was riddled with guilt and needed to confess. I also didn't want the news prompting her to pay Finn another visit to finish what she might have started. "He's a friend of mine. How do you know him?"

"He was in here yesterday with a snap, looking for a relative. After hearing about his accident, I felt awful I hadn't offered to show it to customers and help the lad out. So while in town running errands, I called in to see him and make the offer. As you know, he wasn't in good form."

Her reason for visiting Finn seemed plausible, her concern genuine. The Irish were the nicest and most hospitable people I'd ever met. Except, of course, for the one who'd tried to kill Finn. And she'd seemed frazzled at the hospital compared to her current cool-as-a-cucumber demeanor, whereas my interrogation was making my palms sweat. If I offered to email her the picture, I could gauge her reaction that I had a copy. Yet if I flashed it around, I might once again be putting Finn's life in danger, along with mine.

A guy walked in and grabbed several bags of crisps.

I thanked the woman, and before reaching the door, I turned back to her. "I'm sorry. My name's Mags Murray."

My dad loved the show *Columbo*. Detective Columbo always had one last question or comment prior to leaving, attempting to throw the criminal off his game.

"Stella Connolly. I hope your friend recovers quickly." She turned to her customer. Business as usual.

Either I needed to work on my detective skills, or Stella had perfected her criminal ones.

Or she was innocent.

Or I was investigating a mystery that didn't exist.

Between Finn's warnings and seeing his accident site, I was driving so slowly a tractor was tailgating me. I decided to stop by to visit Edmond as planned, hoping he'd be able to identify the young boys in Finn's photo. If there was one person I could trust besides Biddy, it was Edmond Collier, who'd been sweet on Grandma.

Grandma had taught me that calling on someone unannounced was perfectly acceptable, even neighborly, in her small community. However, showing up without a pie, tart, or biscuits was unheard of. I'd given the ten Christmas puddings to guests, including Edmond, as they'd left the house after the funeral, so I stopped at home and grabbed a pan of lasagna.

One dish down and seventeen to go.

Before leaving the house, I ran to the bathroom. The toilet refused to flush, and a foul odor made my nose crinkle. Lovely. Having little heat was one thing. No toilet quite another. Maybe if I banged the tank with my fist it would flush. More likely the tank would fall off. I could run up to McCarthy's pub during the day, but what about at night? Go in the shrubs behind the house? Maybe Edmond could recommend a cheap plumber.

The elderly man answered the door looking like he'd just rolled out of bed, with unruly tufts of gray hair and dressed in a wrinkled white shirt and blue slacks. He ushered me inside to a living room, where flames danced in a black cast-iron stove, the rustic scent of peat in the air. Several framed vintage photos of nearby villages hung crooked on the cracked plaster walls in desperate need of a fresh coat of white paint. A small, sparse Christmas tree stood in a corner, with an unwrapped present and hundreds of pine needles beneath it.

Had the gift been for Grandma?

Consumed with grief I brushed a finger over my earring —a sterling silver Celtic design with a small emerald. My last Christmas present from Grandma.

Edmond removed stacks of genealogy and history books from a worn blue couch, opening up the only free space in the room for me to sit. He smiled at the pan of lasagna. "Just in time for lunch. I'll heat the oven."

"I already ate, thanks. But you go ahead."

His smile faded, and he took the pan to the kitchen.

I felt horrible lying, but I didn't have time for lunch. I had a week to find a criminal and Finn's father.

Edmond returned from the kitchen with tea and ginger biscuits. An Irish host was always prepared for company. After bringing him up to speed on Finn and his *accident*, I showed him the photo. He plucked a pair of reading glasses from the breast pocket of his wrinkled white shirt and slipped them on.

"1951, maybe 52," he said. "The middle lad has to be Paddy Connolly—can't be more than ten there. Had that same mischievous grin on his face until the day he died. Actually, he might have still been wearing it at his wake."

Connolly?

"Any relation to *Stella* Connolly at the convenience store in Drumcara?"

He nodded. "She owns the place. Was married to Paddy's boy Sean, who passed on a few years before Paddy."

It seemed plausible that Stella hadn't recognized her

father-in-law as a young boy. The only reason I could identify Grandma in her youth was because I'd spent hours poring over her old photo albums. Yet it was awfully coincidental that Stella had shown up at Finn's hospital room when she had a connection to one of the boys in the photo. However, Grandma had insisted that coincidences often happened in genealogy research and led you down the wrong path. Always have more than one source before you validate a clue. But this made me suspicious enough to continue investigating Stella.

"If Paddy was around ten in the photo, he'd be close to eighty if he were alive."

Edmond nodded. "Went to his and his wife Rosie's wedding anniversary at the pub two years back. Funny how fast time goes." He smiled at the photo. "The schoolteacher at the time could likely identify the boys." He massaged his gray stubbly chin. "Would have been Evelyn Mc...something."

"She's still alive?"

He shrugged. "She was two years ago when she attended the school reunion. Lived down in Wicklow. She'd be on your grandma's invite list."

I'd visited Grandma twice during a reunion. I was always the youngest attendee, but I'd loved listening to everyone reminisce about school-day memories.

"I always helped her with the reunion planning," he said. "Can't imagine no more reunions now that she's gone. Sad the way things change." His eyes misted over.

I nodded in agreement. I couldn't imagine no more school reunions, Christmas and summer visits, listening to Grandma's ancestor stories... Panic raced through me. I had to start documenting my family folklore before I forgot it and it was gone forever!

I choked down the lump of emotion in my throat.

"Heard you had an offer on the house," Edmond said.

Was there anyone who hadn't heard about it?

"Haven't accepted it yet. Not sure if they're a good fit." I shared their intended changes.

Edmond shook his head with disapproval. "Would be a shame if they tear down the old stone wall. Would have broken Maggie's heart." He took a deep breath. "I'm sure you'll make the proper decision."

What did he consider the *proper* decision?

I placed a comforting hand on Edmond's. "How about we put that lasagna in the oven?"

He managed a weak smile. "That'd be grand."

Contacting Evelyn McSomething would have to wait. If she was even still alive.

Five

Two hours and three pieces of lasagna later, my jeans button was ready to pop. I promised Edmond I'd return soon for a visit and keep him updated on my research. The prospect of assisting me with a genealogy mystery had put a bounce in his step. He'd also given me the name of a company that could address my toilet issue. I called, and a man promised to send someone out tomorrow afternoon.

What was I supposed to do until then?

Pumping out the septic system would cost two hundred euros, leaving four hundred dollars in my savings. If the toilet still didn't work, they'd have to inspect the system to see if the pumps or pipes needed to be cleaned or replaced. I'd have to put it on my credit card and raise the sale price on the house.

Before heading home to search for the teacher's name and address, I drove ten miles out of my way back to Drumcara for another latte and to visit Stella. It would suck if she were guilty. Not that we'd bonded during my interrogation, but that would mean Finn's dad was dead. That he'd have no hope of getting to know the man or his grandfather.

When I reached Drumcara, my real estate agent called, inquiring about my decision on the Dublin couple's offer. The locals would never forgive me if the old stone wall or fireplace were replaced with brick. I asked him to add to the sales agreement that these features must remain intact. He reluctantly agreed, unsure if the provisions could be enforced. The townspeople would undoubtedly have no problem enforcing them.

No cars sat in the convenience store parking lot. Stella obviously walked to work. I needed to find out what color car she drove. When I entered the shop, I gave her a perky smile. Despite my previous reservations, I decided to mention having a copy of the photo. "You aren't going to believe this. I have a copy of Finn O'Brien's picture, and someone just identified one of the boys as your father-in-law."

Panic flashed in Stella's gray eyes, but she recovered gracefully with a smile. "Really?"

"I was sorry to hear you lost your husband."

She frowned. "I'm sorry to say Paddy couldn't have been the lad's grandfather. My husband Sean was an only child, and we were never blessed with children. It wasn't meant to be."

How did she know Finn was looking for his father? I hadn't mentioned that. On my last visit she'd said Finn had been looking for a *relation*. Maybe Stella hadn't recognized her father-in-law in the photo, but she'd recognized *Finn* when he'd stopped at the store. Maybe he had the same blue eyes as her no-good cheating husband. Maybe Finn walking into the store had added salt to the wound that Stella hadn't been able to have children, but her husband's mistress had. That was a lot of maybes. I felt bad if Stella had unknowingly married some Don Juan, but that didn't justify her possibly having run Finn off the road.

I needed to see a photo of Sean Connolly.

"Not having children allowed us the freedom to travel. We visited every continent except Antarctica. No interest in going someplace with even worse weather than here. Yet Sean wasn't one for lying on the beach and relaxing in the sun." Her gaze darkened, and her grip tightened around a soup can on the counter. "He always complained about the heat. Most would be delighted to get a bit of color on their pale skin. Now that he's gone, my sister and I go to Lanzarote each spring."

From her overly tanned skin, she spent a fair amount of time making up for years of no sunbathing. And that explained her lightweight, colorfully embroidered white cotton shirt, likely purchased at a shop in Portugal. My pale skin was covered with a blue wool sweater and scarf.

"Plan to buy a retirement home there." Thoughts of a blue ocean and sandy beaches perked her up.

Owning a convenience store obviously paid well.

By the time Stella excitedly filled me in on the detailed plans for her beachfront home in the Canary Islands, my latte was gone. I bought another one and told her I'd return for more. She smiled sweetly, but I didn't get an overly excited vibe from her.

I headed across the street to my car, realizing Stella hadn't asked for a copy of Finn's photo to show customers. That was supposedly why she'd driven a half hour to the hospital to visit him. Yet I could have e-mailed her a copy in a matter of seconds, and she hadn't requested one.

Interesting...

I'd parked in front of a yellow pub with a gold-lettered sign reading *O'Sullivan's*. A poster out front advertised an upcoming tractor run. I'd never attended one of the events that benefited local causes or charities. However, Grandma and I had once sat in her front lawn watching hundreds of tractors parade down the road past her house.

Had Finn bought a round of drinks in this pub while showing around his photo? Bartenders were like hairdressers —up on the local gossip and knew everyone. Some bartender in Wyoming was the first person to know about my failed twenty-four-hour engagement. Two a.m. in Ireland, Biddy hadn't answered her phone. That was the summer I'd worked as a lifeguard at Green River Campgrounds and discovered I was allergic to poison oak.

I entered the pub to find a tall white-haired man with a stubbly beard in his late fifties behind an empty bar, watching a priest throw darts. You didn't see that every day. Father threw three bull's-eyes in a row and left.

"Comes in every day after confession," the bartender said. "Guess it's a stress reliever."

"He's quite good. Obviously has a lot of stress to relieve."

George O'Sullivan and I exchanged introductions.

His yellow sports jersey had the number 77 across the front encircled with *Bad Reputation* on top and *Lynott* beneath. "Is Lynott a rugby or hurling player?"

He laughed. "I'll let that one go seeing as you're a Yank," he said good naturedly. The Irish term of endearment for people from the States. "Phil Lynott was the lead singer of Thin Lizzy, one of the most popular bands to come out of Ireland. They released the album *Bad Reputation* in 1977."

I nodded despite being unfamiliar with the band.

His gaze narrowed. "'The Boys are Back in Town'?"

"Oh, I know that song." My dad listened to classic rock.

"Aye, there's hope for ya yet." His look turned serious. "Not being local, ya best be careful now driving on these roads. Had a bad accident on one right outside of town two days ago. The lad had been in here just before."

I feigned surprise, slipping onto a barstool. "How awful. Was he from around here?"

"Not sure from whereabouts he hailed. Had a snap of the Ballycaffey schoolhouse. Was wondering if I recognized several young lads in it."

I wanted to ask if Finn had disclosed his connection to one of the boys, and also for a list of who'd been here that day but who might seem a bit too curious.

"Me being from Mayo, I didn't recognize 'em. Just helping out here while my brother Brody is on holiday in Spain." He gestured to a framed photo hanging behind the bar of two young boys in sports uniforms holding hurling sticks—George and his brother, I assumed. Besides the photo, framed vintage posters hung on the wall. One with a toucan boasting the health benefits of Guinness. Another with a dog balancing a glass of whiskey on its snout. Apparently, animals sold alcohol.

I nodded toward the convenience store across the street. "How long has Stella run the store?"

"As long as I can remember. Sean bought it shortly after they were married. To keep her busy when he was out of town. He was an airline pilot. A good-looking fella. Rather than a girl in every port, he'd had a girl in every *air*port." He chuckled at his play on the cliched expression.

No doubt Stella hadn't found it funny. And likely hadn't been ignorant to her husband's affairs, if this guy from Mayo knew about them. Sean had been what my grandma would have called a skirt chaser. Maybe Stella hadn't cared to know if Finn was the result of one of those skirts.

"Sorry. Shouldn't be talking that way about the dead. Merely repeating a bit of gossip I once heard."

"So he was gone a lot?"

George shrugged. "A few years back when I was tending bar, he sounded like he did loads of trips to England and quick jaunts to the continent."

Had the man hooked up with Finn's mom in that Liverpool hotel on one of his layovers? Enquiring if Sean had been a pilot in 1990 might also seem a bit too curious.

"Our specialty is Guinness stew. My own recipe."

Still stuffed, I ordered a bag of crisps and a hot tea to go, already having finished my second latte. I'd be wide awake at 2:00 a.m.

"Looks like Stella got her car back," George said.

I followed his gaze out the window to Stella getting into a small *red* car parked in front of a white townhouse. "Where was it?"

"In getting fixed. Said someone backed into her."

Or she'd run someone off the road two days ago?

"How bad was the damage?"

"Didn't see it."

If Stella was responsible for Finn's accident, the evidence was gone.

I thanked George for the tea and conversation. He'd been more helpful than he realized.

The pub sat at a crossroads. I peered down the four roads, wondering which one Finn had taken into Drumcara and which pubs he'd stopped at along the way to question patrons. George had told him about the schoolhouse's location, which led me to believe Finn hadn't come from Ballycaffey. However, I decided to go back that way.

When I arrived in Ballycaffey, I parked in front of a large yellow building with a green-lettered sign reading *Casey's*. The pub had closed after the owner, Christopher Casey, died five years ago. Nobody had bought it, due to the recession and stiffer drunk-driving laws.

The convenience store across the street was set to reopen next month following renovations from water damage. However, the post office inside it would remain closed due to a nationwide restructuring plan that was shutting down over 150 post offices, mainly rural. Grandma had complained about that at length. The takeaway place, which didn't open until three, only had room out front for the clerk and one customer. The gas station was the only business currently open in the morning. Quite depressing that Ballycaffey had become a bit of a ghost town.

The building that housed Charlotte's Café had remained vacant since Charlotte passed away four years ago at ninety-two. Grandma had made pies and tarts for the restaurant for forty years until she'd retired five years ago. Her baked goods were famous for miles. I would keep her recipes but had little hope of being able to duplicate her tasty desserts. In her teens, my mom had waitressed at the café, saving money to get out of the *hick* town. She'd always claimed I'd inherited her wanderlust. Yet she'd moved to Chicago and rarely traveled farther than the burbs. My passion for travel had to have come from my biological father.

A man walked out of the gas station next to where I was standing in front of the empty building. He was seventyish with thick silver hair, a five-o'clock shadow, and blue eyes.

"Looking for a shop, are ya?" he asked me.

"Ah, no, but thank you."

His smile sparked a twinkle in his bright-blue eyes. He looked vaguely familiar. I continued staring as he hopped into his truck, probably thinking I was totally daft. He waved and drove off. He was miles down the road when it finally hit me.

He had Finn's eyes.

Or possibly Finn had *his* eyes.

After just having encountered the blond mystery woman from Finn's hospital room earlier this morning, could I have been lucky enough to have run across his father?

The entire way home I kicked myself for not having written down that man's license plate number. Gray was likely the most common vehicle color in Ireland. And maybe he'd merely been passing through from a nearby town. I could spend days driving around searching for gray trucks, when I wouldn't know one from the other.

Hopefully, our paths would cross again.

When I pulled in the drive, the sheep with pink markings

glanced up from an aluminum pan on the front stoop, a glob of mashed potatoes on his black nose. My stomach growled despite being full. Mashed potatoes were my favorite. I lay on the horn. He slid an annoyed glance my way, then gave the pan one last lick before trotting off. Not only had he devoured the contents but also the foil that had undoubtedly covered the top. I headed inside with the empty pan.

A shiver raced through me. It wasn't much warmer inside than it was outside. Remembering to build a fire before leaving the house was difficult when I'd been brought up to not even leave candles burning unattended. Once I lit a roaring fire, I went upstairs to look for the reunion's invite list.

After an hour of searching every binder, box, and envelope, I found it in the last place I'd expected. An Excel document on Grandma's old computer. Wow. Grandma had been more techie than I'd given her credit for. There were three Evelyns on the list but only one in Wicklow—Evelyn McCreery.

I phoned the woman, who confirmed she'd taught school here for twenty-eight years, starting in 1949. E-mailing her a copy of Finn's photo wasn't an option since she didn't own a computer. However, she said it would be lovely to have company, so I scheduled a visit for the following day. She lived a half hour south of Dublin, about an hour-and-a-half drive. I didn't want to get my hopes up too high that she'd recall four of the hundreds of students she'd taught over the years, especially sixty years ago. They would have been some of her first pupils.

A collage on the office's lavender wall displayed a half dozen photos of former students at school reunions. Faces were too small to tell if any resembled the boys in Finn's picture. Edmond had pegged Paddy Connolly merely from his mischievous grin. I smiled at a reunion shot taken five years ago. Seventy-two of us stood in front of the house huddled under umbrellas. My windblown hair had whipped against my face, while Grandma's beautician had firmly sprayed her tight gray curls so even gale-force winds wouldn't have loosened them. We'd moved the outdoor party to McCarthy's pub. Biddy and I had helped her father bartend, amazed at how much alcohol the elderly group had consumed.

Sitting at the desk, I paged through the roster. In 1951, Paddy Connolly had attended school along with thirty-two other boys. It didn't note students' grade levels, merely their ages. Grandma had compiled the list for reunion purposes, including death dates, occupations, and emigrations. I'd once viewed the original rosters dated 1876 to 1980 now on file at the Ballycaffey school. Sadly, it didn't include students' parents' names, but it provided other helpful research information, such as a student's age, residence location, parents' occupation, religious affiliation, and often the name of a previous school. Knowing a child's previous school helped a genealogist locate birth records for children born elsewhere.

The rosters also provided family information that had been lost due to Ireland's censuses being destroyed over the years. The 1821 to 1851 censuses were lost in the 1922 fire at Dublin's Public Record Office at the onset of the Civil War. Since the 1901 Census was the earliest to survive, genealogists had to be quite resourceful. I'd helped Grandma search temporary fever hospitals' registers, wage ledgers, convict lists, and even dog license registrations that went back to

1810. Interesting that the country registered dogs ten years before they began registering people.

A former student's framed sketch of the schoolhouse hung on the wall. Grandma had also made prints. If Evelyn didn't have one, she'd surely appreciate the gesture. I found an extra print in the desk's bottom drawer, along with photo stock paper. I printed off a half dozen copies of Finn's photo.

The doorbell rang.

I went downstairs to find Biddy rather than more casseroles. She breezed inside wearing her green fleece rugby jacket over an orange Scooby Doo nurse's uniform. She tossed glossy brochures for a Greek Isles cruise onto the cocktail table. "Finally booked my parents' thirty-fifth anniversary trip in April. The itinerary is brill. It starts and ends in Venice. How romantic is that? Departing and arriving Venice via the waterways. Thanks again for contributing."

"Of course."

Biddy's parents were my second parents. Our moms had been close friends in school. That was how Biddy and I'd met and become fast friends. After moving to Chicago, my mom returned to Ireland less and less. Biddy's mom and my mom grew apart, whereas Biddy and I grew closer. After getting my DNA results, I'd questioned Biddy's mom about my biological father's identity, hoping my mom had confided in her.

She hadn't.

"Clare still hasn't forked over her share." Biddy rolled her eyes. "Thankfully, my auntie Marie paid for half. The only bad part will be me having to bartend that weekend. Nobody better be giving me a hard time at closing."

A picture of the blue Aegean Sea against a landscape of

white buildings lulled me into Zen mode. The blue reminded me of Finn's eyes. "Maybe I should get a gig working a Mediterranean cruise."

I could always add it to my around-the-world bucket list from the sale of Grandma's house. I needed to start planning my yearlong trip if I wanted to embark on my adventure this summer. My first stop would be Paris to visit Pére Lachaise cemetery and snap a pic of Jim Morrison's grave for my dad, a huge Doors fan. The place looked like a museum, with all its statues and ornate gravestones. Many of my Irish ancestors had been able to only afford wooden crosses on their graves. People had long ago stolen them for firewood.

I'd tracked down Biddy at the hospital and told her about Finn's second warning. She'd agreed I should contact the police.

"The officer didn't feel that Finn telling me to be careful constituted a warning. Doubt she'll be following up on it unless Finn wakes up and... I can't believe I just said *unless* he wakes up."

"Stay positive. He'll be grand. I checked in with his nurse before leaving, and no change. Not worse anyway."

I filled her in on my encounter with Stella.

"Her story sounds a bit fishy, going to see him about showing around his snap. She bloody well ran him off the road—ya know it."

I nodded. "Something's not right, that's for sure."

"Can't picture the woman. Rarely go the Drumcara way to work. Will have to pay Stella a visit. I got on quite well with Paddy Connolly. He always stopped in the pub after coming in from the fields. His wife, Rosie, would ring my dad to send him home for dinner. We should call in on her."

"Under what pretense?"

"That Edmond mentioned it's Paddy in the lovely snap you found in your granny's belongings. That you thought she might be liking a copy. Maybe she'll recognize the other three lads."

"And then I won't have to drive to Wicklow." I told her about my planned visit with Evelyn McCreery tomorrow. "I could also say I'm updating the reunion's student roster with additional family information, like if her sons happened to be in Liverpool, January 8, 1990. The only clue about Finn's father we have to go on."

"Shame on you—lying to the woman about having a reunion."

"Just because I'm selling the house doesn't mean I can't hold a reunion this summer in my grandma's memory. Can have it at your pub and come here for photos."

"Unless the new owners won't be allowing people on their front lawn to take snaps."

"I'll write that into the sales agreement, along with the stone wall and fireplace. Which reminds me. I haven't heard from my real estate agent if the Dublin couple agreed to the stipulations."

"I'd take that as a no." Biddy sprang up from the couch. "Let's pay Rosie a visit."

"You go home and change. I'll pop by after I visit my grandma's grave to tell her about Finn. Let's hope Stella hasn't already told Rosie about seeing Finn's photo."

"If she's responsible for Finn's accident, I think she'll be keeping her gob shut. And I'll be going with ya to Wicklow tomorrow. After Finn's warning, you need to stop snooping around by yourself. I don't want you being brought by ambulance into the hospital."

That made two of us.

Biddy gestured to her uniform. "We're a bit like Velma and Daphne trying to solve a mystery."

More like Shaggy and Scooby.

Six

THE CEMETERY WAS LOCATED down a narrow rural road at the site of an abandoned medieval church. At the back, weathered gravestones and Celtic crosses covered in ivy and moss stood stoically on uneven ground. Grandma and Grandpa were buried there near her parents and grandparents. A massive wrought-iron gate with spear-tipped posts allowed entrance through a towering stone wall covered with overgrown thorny bushes and hedges. A layer of pebbles or colored glass chippings covered the more level ground in front of many of the newer graves toward the front. An Irish tradition. Evergreen wreaths, small mangers, Santa figurines, and miniature Christmas trees decorated both older and newer graves. Another tradition.

Passing by a grave, a tombstone caught my eye.

Paddy and Rosie Connolly. Her death date pending. Next to it a headstone for their son Sean and his wife Stella, her death date also TBD. No way was that woman planning to have her remains shipped from the Canary Islands back to Ireland. I wanted to tell Rosie to sell Stella's plot and use the extra cash to throw herself the wake of the century. Better than Stella selling it to put a new deck on her Lanzarote retirement home.

I peered at Sean's headstone. "Were you unfaithful on January 8, 1990, in Liverpool?"

Too bad I couldn't flat out ask that question to all of Finn's potential fathers. After what happened to Finn, I needed to tread lightly. If people felt interrogated, they might not even share the tiniest clues. And it wasn't fair to Finn's father if everyone in town knew about his son possibly before he did. It was his business, and nobody else's. If Finn's accident likely hadn't been an *accident*, I didn't want to flash the photo around and give families a heads-up and have them clam up. And *I* didn't want to have an accident.

A small artificial tree decorated with ornaments sat in front of both graves as well as the one next to them, David and Nora Reilly. Were the families related?

I smiled at my memory of David and Nora's grave. An irreverent reaction considering Biddy had fallen through the grave when we were ten.

When Grandma had conducted cemetery research, Biddy and I often tagged along and made crayon rubbings of old tombstone inscriptions. Grandma had warned us that it was bad luck to step on a grave. It was nearly impossible not to with the close quarters of the gravesites, so Biddy and I'd made a game of it.

Biddy had jumped from the stone border outlining one side of the Reillys' grave to the other. When she landed, her foot slipped back and broke through the thin layer of pebble and concrete mixture, continuing down to the sunken earth below. Biddy went hysterical, certain her foot had smashed through a decomposing coffin to a dead body. I'd wrapped my arms around her upper body and heaved backward, hoisting her up onto solid ground as Grandma came dashing over. When Grandma saw what had happened, she frantically made the sign of the cross, worried we'd upset the grave. Not nearly as worried about poor Biddy.

When we dropped Biddy off at the pub, her mom and two patrons were inside. Biddy stripped off her jeans and tennies right there in the pub and whipped them into the roaring fire. I could still smell the burning rubber soles to this day.

Grandma paid for the grave's repairs and made us promise never to repeat Biddy's claim that her foot had gone through the coffin. Since that traumatic day, Biddy hadn't entered a cemetery.

Leaving the newer section behind, I traipsed through the tall grass covering a sloping hill toward Grandma's grave. I touched my foot cautiously on the ground before placing my weight on it, not wanting to trip on a toppled-over tombstone or get sucked into a sinkhole like Biddy had. Solar twinkle lights covered Grandma and Grandpa's granite tombstone, whereas moss and ivy blanketed her parents' and grandparents' stones.

I spied Edmond sitting on a mound of dirt next to Grandma's grave. I cringed at the thought of the elderly man navigating the treacherous terrain. Should I leave, not wishing to disturb his visit, or stay to help him return safely to even ground? Before I could decide, he waved me over. Dressed in a pressed navy suit, spiffed up for Grandma, he had a glass of whiskey in his hand, a bottle at his feet. Several ginger biscuits and a whiskey sat by Grandma's tombstone. A nightly nip had helped her sleep.

I swallowed the lump of emotion in my throat. "Sorry. didn't mean to interrupt. I'll come back later."

Edmond managed a faint smile, a slight sparkle in his misty eyes. "Nonsense. Join us. Plenty of biscuits for everyone. Sorry, I don't have an extra glass."

"No worries."

"Was just telling Maggie about the exciting genealogy case we're working on."

I brought Edmond and Grandma up to speed on everything that had occurred since my visit with him.

"I'm going to see Evelyn McCreery tomorrow. I'll let you know the outcome."

"If I didn't have a doctor's appointment, I'd be more than happy to join ya."

"Once we identify the four families, we can call in on them."

"Ah, that'd be grand. Also mentioned to Maggie that you had an offer on the house. Sorry. That really wasn't my news to share."

"I stipulated in the sales agreement that the stone wall and fireplace must remain intact."

"Brilliant idea." He smiled wide, turning to the grave. "Did ya be hearing that, Maggie? The buyers agreed to keeping the wall."

They hadn't actually agreed yet. I wasn't selling unless they did.

"I recall helping her plant the trellis rose bush when Liam passed away." He massaged his stubbly chin, a reminiscent glint in his gray eyes. "Your grandfather built the trellis, ya know."

I shook my head. I hadn't known that, but he'd been an incredible woodworker. He'd also constructed the rocking chair in the living room, which I planned to keep. Grandpa died when I was four. Grandma's stories and photos provided my only memories of the short man always wearing a smile.

"I'll make sure the rosebush stays," I said.

No way was that couple replacing Grandpa's memorial with a brick wall. However, since they hadn't yet agreed to retaining the stone wall and fireplace, they'd unlikely agree to the trellis.

Then I'd find someone who would.

Biddy hadn't recalled seeing Rosie Connolly at Grandma's wake, so I didn't have to worry about being embarrassed if I regifted her casserole. I selected a chicken curry dish from the shed. If it warmed up much more outside, I'd have to start eating casseroles for breakfast or do more socializing to give away the sixteen dishes remaining in the shed, fridge, and freezer.

I turned to Biddy behind the wheel. "Did you know that Connollys are related to Patrick and Nora Reilly?"

Biddy's eyes about bugged out of her head. "How do you know they're related?"

"When I visited my grandma's grave, I noticed Paddy's and Sean's graves were decorated with the same Christmas tree as the Reillys'. Edmond was there and confirmed they were Rosie's parents."

"Janey Mac!" Biddy smacked a palm against the steering wheel. "I hadn't a clue. Rosie and Paddy were always nice to me after the incident."

"I doubt my grandma told them the entire story."

"Why'd you just tell *me* they're related?" Biddy scratched nervously at her neck as she pulled up the drive to the Connollys' white bungalow.

"Sorry." I slapped Biddy's hand away from her neck. "Stop scratching. If Rosie thinks you've broken out in hives, she won't let us in the house."

"Maybe I have and it's contagious. Don't want to be giving it to an elderly lady. I best—"

"Shut your yap."

A defeated groan vibrated at the back of her throat. "Fine."

No doorbell, I rapped on the blue wooden door.

Rosie answered wearing a bright smile. With her perfectly coifed short white hair, porcelain skin, and pink apron covering her blue and pink floral-patterned dress, she looked like she'd just stepped out of a 1950s family TV show. She ushered us inside, the scent of fresh-baked goods filling the air.

She led us into a sitting room with gray furnishings and light-blue walls. "Have a seat. Dinner is almost ready." She whisked out of the room.

"Dinner?" Biddy and I muttered.

Biddy continued scratching her neck. "She forgave me for falling through her parents' grave—she'll surely forgive us for skipping dinner."

"We aren't skipping dinner and upsetting her." I spied a yellowed black-and-white newspaper clipping of Finn's photo framed on top of the piano. "Well, looky here." I walked over to it. No names were noted under the photo. "Unless Stella has an incredibly poor memory or has never visited her in-laws, she *had* known her father-in-law was one of the boys in the photo." I wanted to pop over to Drumcara and tell the woman, "Liar liar pants on fire." Yet I didn't want to tip her off that I'd discovered she'd known at least one boy's identity.

"What valid reason could she have had to lie about the photo other than running Finn off the road?" Biddy said.

I nodded. "Had she known her husband Sean had an affair, or had she merely come unhinged over the prospect of it?"

Rosie breezed into the room, and Biddy and I jumped. "Sorry. Didn't mean to be startling you. I'm sure you recognize the home in that snap."

"Do you know any of the boys besides Paddy?" I asked.

"Unfortunately not. I hailed from County Cork."

Road trip tomorrow to Wicklow to visit Evelyn McCreery.

"Should have had Paddy write the lads' names on the back."

I couldn't count how many times Grandma had said the same thing when searching through people's old family photos. Yet she'd also found it upsetting when people wrote a person's name in ink across their forehead. I'd love to have the four boys' names written on the photo, unless it obstructed their faces.

"My grandma had copies of the original photo if you'd like one."

Rosie placed a hand to her chest. "Aw, that'd be grand. Paddy's mum might have had the snap, but the family albums went to his sister."

Family vacation photos also filled the piano top.

"It that Neuschwanstein Castle?" I asked. The Bavarian fairy-tale castle was on my bucket list.

Rosie nodded. "Paddy's mum had German roots. Took a holiday there once hoping to find family, without any success."

"Do you know the surname?"

She shook her head. "Don't recall. Come. Dinner is ready." She whisked off.

"Good to know Paddy had German ancestry on his maternal side if Finn's new DNA test shows German ethnicity. His paternal test had a Burkhardt match, which sounds German but can't be a maternal connection. Coincidences always keep genealogists on their toes."

Biddy nodded at Stella and Sean's wedding photo. "And Finn has Sean's dark hair and build."

Finn's dreamy blue eyes didn't stare back at me from Sean's photo. Maybe it hadn't captured their true color.

We joined Rosie in the dining room, straight out of a *Better Homes and Gardens* magazine. A long mahogany table was set with fine china, silver serving dishes and utensils, and Waterford crystal glasses. Each plate had a helping of roasted potatoes, mashed potatoes, cooked baby carrots, and a slice of meat covered with a brown sauce that looked and smelled suspiciously like lamb. My stomach tossed.

Had my dislike of lamb heightened my fear of sheep?

Rosie sat at the head of the table, while Biddy and I took a seat on each side of her.

"It looks delicious, but you didn't have to go to all this trouble," I said.

"Nonsense, luv. I so miss cooking for a family. My mum was a brilliant cook. Knew a dozen different ways to make potatoes, and this is her secret sauce on the lamb."

I choked back an involuntary gag at the mention of lamb. Biddy scratched her neck like a dog with fleas at the thought of Rosie's mother's grave. I shot her a stern look. She reluctantly lowered her hand.

"I met your daughter-in-law Stella," I told Rosie.

The woman's smile faded; her soft features hardened. "How's she getting on?" She stabbed a small roasted potato with a fork.

"Not sure," I said. "Just popped in for a latte when I was driving through Drumcara."

"Indeed, they make a lovely coffee." Rosie's smile returned. "Haven't had one in a while."

Did that mean she hadn't seen Stella recently?

Rosie gazed out a large picture window at the green fields and rolling hills, where sheep and cows had likely once grazed. "This will all be hers one day. It was Sean's wish." She frowned. "That woman never wanted children. I don't care what she says, she didn't. Would have meant sharing her inheritance with someone."

Stella had given me the impression she'd wanted children. If Sean had been an only child with none of his own, that meant Stella inherited everything. Another reason for her to want Finn dead. That must be how Stella could afford a retirement home in the Canary Islands. I didn't have the heart to tell poor Rosie that was Stella's plan and that she'd also likely sell her burial plot. What a horrible thing to do. To sell the land your husband's family had farmed for generations.

Yet I was selling Grandma's house. However, generations of Flanagans had never lived in the house or on that same land. Yet still, many of my ancestors had attended school in the house. Did that make me no better than Stella?

"Was such a shame I couldn't make it to your grandmother's wake or funeral. Haven't been in good form. A flu bug. And will be sad to see the school reunions end. Haven't missed a one even though I didn't attend school there. It's great fun and lovely to hear people's memories of Paddy. It's like he's still here with me. You know Paddy's grandfather built the stone wall out back and the fireplace. He was quite the stone mason. Paddy always appreciated Maggie taking such good care of the wall."

Good thing I'd already added saving the fireplace and wall to the sales agreement.

"I plan to hold a reunion this summer in my grandma's memory."

"Ah, that's splendid, isn't it now?" Rosie stood up. "So sorry. I forgot the wine."

As soon as Rosie left the room, I speared the slice of lamb with a fork and dropped it onto Biddy's plate.

"What are ya doing? I can't be eating all of that."

"Me throwing up on Rosie's fine china would certainly be more offensive to the woman than you accidentally falling through her parents' grave. We can't upset her."

Biddy was about to dispute my claim, when Rosie

returned with *two* bottles of red wine. Holy cats. How long did she plan on us staying?

During dinner, Rosie reminisced affectionately about her son Sean having flown for Aer Lingus since the late 1980s, mainly short-haul flights between Ireland and the UK. He'd taken her on exotic trips to Paris, Florence, and Barcelona.

"I once joined him and Stella on a holiday in Portugal. Stella had insisted on window shopping for real estate, when Sean had no desire to purchase a holiday home outside Ireland. This led to a brutal argument, which put me in quite an awkward position. I never traveled with the two of them again. Actually, following that trip they began taking separate holidays."

I was starting to wonder if Sean had died under suspicious circumstances. Like if he'd been run off the road by a little red car. I had the feeling Stella was much happier now than during their marriage.

Rosie eyed Biddy's half-eaten dinner with concern. "You don't like lamb, luv?"

Biddy nodded enthusiastically. "It's grand. Just a bit full. Sorry." She gave me the evil eye.

"Well, even if you can't finish dinner, you must have room for apple tart." Rosie glanced over at me. "Of course, it could never compare to your grandmother's tart."

I smiled at the thought of Grandma's strawberry rhubarb tart. My favorite. Maybe I'd have to give the recipe a try.

Biddy looked like she was going to be ill.

"I'm afraid we're going to have to pass," I said. "We have to be on the road to Wicklow early in the morning."

Rosie frowned. "No worries. I understand."

We thanked Rosie for a lovely dinner and promised to

stop by for dessert another time. We hopped into Biddy's car and sped off.

"See, that wasn't so bad," I said. "She doesn't hold a grudge about her parents' graves. Wasn't worth scratching your neck raw over."

"And Stella knew darn well that was Paddy in Finn's photo. She definitely ran Finn off the road, so Sean is likely Finn's father."

"Or Stella lost it at the mere thought of Sean having an illegitimate son who could destroy her plans for a retirement home in the Canary Islands."

"People have killed for a lot less. Like the woman in Donegal who stabbed her husband for eating the last piece of tea cake. Must have been a *killer* cake." Biddy let out a nervous giggle, which grew into hysterical laughter. She had to pull over and get a grip.

Reliving her traumatic experience with the Reillys' grave had taken its toll on poor Biddy.

When I got home, red embers still glowed in the cast-iron stove. It wasn't exactly warm inside, but at least I wasn't shivering. I threw a few more peat logs onto the fire.

My phone rang. My sister Emma.

A sense of dread crept over me, like the Grim Reaper had just pounded on my door.

I reluctantly answered the call, and we exchanged hellos.

"Dad mentioned you had an offer on the house."

Emma's chipper tone was my first clue something was up. She was so not a bubbly person. Precisely why her and

Dread Ted were the perfect couple. I'd given him the nick-name the first time we'd met. The man had zero personality, and I always dreaded having to visit with him. Emma and him discussing their finance jobs was as mind numbing as listening to my sister Mia drone on about her cooking shows. She was constantly sending me recipes, knowing I don't cook.

Neither of my older sisters had ever asked me about my travels!

I took a calming breath. "Both the funeral and wake went fine, thanks."

"Yeah, Dad mentioned they had."

How about asking for yourself? Or sending flowers to the funeral? Dad had sent an arrangement of peonies, Grandma's favorite, and had checked on me several times over the past week. At least he'd had a valid excuse for not making the funeral, having been in Australia for his architectural business.

"I haven't heard back from the buyers."

"Heard back about what? Thought it was a done deal?"

"They're considering a few of the provisions."

"Like what?" Her tone went from cheerful to fearful in a matter of one sentence.

I told her about the items I'd added to the agreement.

"That's insane, Mags. You can't expect people to keep the house as is. It'll be their house. They can make any changes they want."

"I'm not arguing about it."

"Of course not—it's always about what *you* want."

I sprang from the couch, my grip tightening around the phone. "Like how *I* wanted to visit Grandma every summer, and you didn't? Like *I* wanted to spend Christmas with her? Like *I* wanted to listen to all her stories about our ancestors, when you didn't care to listen to even one?" I paced the living room, pointing at myself as if she could see me. "If it's always about what *I* want, then I shouldn't have said I'd consider giving you a share of the sale."

She gasped. "That's not fair."

"Fine. If you can tell me Grandma's parents' names or the story about how she and Grandpa met, I'll give you a share of the sale."

Silence filled the line.

"I didn't think so."

Click. I disconnected the call, turned off my phone, and whipped it to the loveseat cushions. Had I just informed her she wasn't receiving a dime from the sale?

I marched into the kitchen and poured a whiskey. I took a drink, gagged, and dumped it out. If ever there were a time I could have tolerated the liquor, this would have been it.

I went upstairs and changed into jammies. My velour robe lay in a pile on the unmade bed. After slipping on the robe, I tucked in the white sheets and spread the green floral duvet across the double bed. I couldn't sleep in an unmade bed even if it meant making it right before hopping in.

The light green duvet matched the walls to a tee. Vintage family photos and ones of Grandma and me during our travels around Ireland sat on top of two white nightstands and an armoire. The chest held my clothes I kept here.

I turned off the light, and the moon shone through the small window in the slanted roof. It was merely to let in the sunshine, not the fresh air. I'd once opened it to air out the upstairs and was attacked by an army of flies waiting on the roof for some shmuck to unwittingly let them in. The surrounding field of cows and the warm tile roof attracted them.

An hour later, I was sipping tea in front of the fireplace, documenting one of Grandma's school-day memories. When she was thirteen, the boys' hurling team made it to the finals for the first time, playing against their biggest rivalry, Kinneboggen. Down a player on gameday, and desperate not to forfeit, the boys had convinced Grandma to fill in. Grandma had been the top player on the camogie team— woman's hurling. She cut her hair, hid her not-yet-fully-developed woman's body beneath a large jersey, and helped lead the boys' team to victory. Go Grandma!

I didn't inherit her athletic abilities.

Unless, of course, I was highly motivated, like being chased by a sheep.

The wind picked up, pelting rain against the windows— making me have to pee. It was 11:00 p.m. Biddy was likely still up. I slipped on my wellies and dashed through the rain to my car. I drove up to Biddy's. Nobody answered the door. I jumped back into the car and parked out front. I zipped inside McCarthy's pub, where Biddy's dad was talking to two older men at the bar. They eyed my interesting outfit.

"Just using the loo," I said, flying past them.

They all nodded and returned to their conversation.

Any embarrassment over wearing my robe and jammies to the pub paled in comparison to my infamous sheep incident when I was ten.

Seven

THE FOLLOWING MORNING, Biddy and I were on our way to Evelyn McCreery's with Finn's photo, a sketch of the schoolhouse, a ham and cabbage dish, and lemon bread. I'd also brought the school roster. If Evelyn identified the boys, I could verify they'd been students.

"You know it's eighty here?" Biddy gestured to the cars speeding past me on the motorway around Dublin.

"You're the one who told me to drive carefully. That you didn't want to see me in the emergency room."

"You're more likely to be *causing* an accident driving like my granny. It's gorgeous out. Not like it's lashing rain and ya can't be seeing the road."

"Do you want to drive?"

"No. You need the practice, never having driven around Dublin. I'll drive back though since I'd like to be in bed before midnight."

I rolled my eyes.

Just south of Dublin, a green mountain range welcomed us to County Wicklow. The Wicklow Mountains were more like exceptionally large hills rather than the rugged Rockies in the western US. Tree foliage canopied much of the county's rural winding roads.

Grandma and I'd once traveled the entire length of the county down to Avoca Valley to conduct genealogy research. When I'd returned home from Ireland, my mom's friend, who'd recently visited Wicklow, asked me what I'd found most interesting. Shopping for colorful woolen goods at the original Avoca store, touring Powerscourt Estate, or visiting the popular monastic site, Glendalough.

I'd replied that I'd been fascinated by the number of illegitimate children documented in the 1800s baptismal records. And that Grandma had attributed this to the county's southeast area having been a big mining community with a lot of single men or married ones, who'd left home to find work. This had likely led to the establishment of brothels.

Mom and her friend had stared at me in horror. A twelve-year-old girl shouldn't have known about such scandalous things. Later that evening I overheard Mom on the phone scolding Grandma for taking me to such a place. That *place* having been an Irish Catholic church, not a house of ill repute. Next time I'd visited Grandma, I'd promised to never again share our adventures with my mother.

We now exited the motorway and encountered winding roads canopied with trees. After passing through a quaint village, I turned down a one-lane road with grass growing up the center. My grip tightened on the steering wheel. The roads by Grandma's were child's play compared to this one. Every so often a small patch of shoulder appeared, in case you encountered another vehicle, which hopefully wasn't a tractor.

Thankfully, Evelyn's was right around the bend or I'd have walked the rest of the way. I parked in the dirt drive in front of the white thatched-roof cottage. A purple door and lime-green window boxes matched the trim and doors on two stone outbuildings. A brightly painted cobblestone path led to the house, where an orange cat sunbathed in a window box. Evelyn—a tall, trim elderly woman—answered the door with a welcoming smile. Aqua-colored paint blemished her pale cheek and speckled her long silver hair.

"Ah, so lovely to have visitors." She wiped her hands on her faded jeans before giving our cheeks a pinch. "Please come in."

She ushered us down a lavender-painted hallway with brightly painted furnishings. The scent of fresh paint rather than baked goods filled the air. The yellow living room was in the process of being painted the aqua color on Evelyn's cheek. A drop cloth covered the floor and outlined the shapes of three pet beds beneath. Cats had instinctively located their beds and were lying in them sunning themselves in front of a patio door. Evelyn thanked me for the dish and peeked under the foil covering the aluminum pan. The cats' eyes shot open, their noses twitching at the smell of ham and cabbage.

A smile brightened Evelyn's face. "Oh my, doesn't that look tasty." She peered over at her roomies. "Come, lads. See what these nice ladies have brought us." She removed the foil and set the pan on the floor.

The cats sprang from their beds and began feasting on the ham and cabbage. Biddy and I exchanged amused smiles, taking a seat on the couch.

"I also brought some lemon bread." I set the platter of sliced bread on the yellow cocktail table with purple legs.

We were not sharing it with the cats.

"But I'm sorry if we came at a bad time." I glanced around at the painting in progress.

"Nonsense, luv. I'm always painting something." Evelyn went out to the front entry. Moments later the cat from the window box joined the others.

She returned with a pot of tea and eyed the nearly empty pan on the floor. "Now don't be making piggies out of yourselves. Leave some for me." She set the pan on a high shelf next to a collection of colorful ceramic sheep.

The cats returned to their beds in the sun, along with the newcomer finding a spot on the drop cloth.

I'd worked one summer at the Kitty Kafé in Seattle. Patrons could lounge on couches and chairs or comfy Berber cushions, which resembled cat beds. Customers' food was served in large ceramic cat feeding dishes. Climbing trees and perches lined the front windows, allowing the residents to sun themselves.

Evelyn sat in a red upholstered chair next to us, and I presented her the schoolhouse sketch.

She admired it. "How lovely. Did you draw this yourself, luv?"

I felt like one of her students. "Ah, no, someone drew it at one of the school reunions."

She nodded faintly, no glint of recognition in her pale-blue eyes.

"At the *Ballycaffey* schoolhouse where you taught. I think you attended a reunion there a few years ago."

Evelyn's gaze narrowed on the drawing for the longest time. Then her eyes widened. "My, yes, that is the schoolhouse." She shook her head. "After thirty-seven years teaching, you'd certainly think I'd have recognized it."

Oh boy. If she hadn't recognized the school, she was never going to remember four of the hundreds of students she'd taught. I was a bit hesitant to show her Finn's photo, not wanting to upset her if she couldn't identify the boys.

"The schoolhouse." Her eyes teared up. "Oh, that's lovely, isn't it?" She gave my hand a squeeze. "Forgot you mentioned on the phone that you're Maggie's granddaughter."

She'd let me in the house without remembering who I was? That was a bit unsafe. Her recognizing the school was a good sign, so I took the plunge and showed her Finn's photo.

"These boys were your students around 1950."

She slipped on a pair of glasses and squinted at the photo. Hopefully, it was crisp enough for her to make out their faces. Biddy and I exchanged nervous glances while she studied it.

She shook a disapproving finger at the boy on the left. "Mickey Molloy. The reason I decided not to have children, he was. Oh, the shenanigans that lad got himself into. Once let a ferret in the schoolhouse. The poor animal was scared half to death, as was I."

I'd read about that incident in Grandma's school journal.

"Kicked a soccer ball through the back window one time and blamed it on his friend..." She tapped a finger against her thin lips. "Paddy Connolly. Might be him there with that mischievous grin on his face. Saw him at a reunion a few years back. Hadn't changed a bit."

I didn't want to be the one to tell her he'd passed away.

"Taught Paddy's son Sean also. Always thought he

looked so much like his father. Not possible of course, seeing as he was adopted."

That would throw a wrench in Finn's DNA test, unless they exhumed Sean's body, which Stella would never approve. And I wasn't adding grave robber to my list of shenanigans.

I discreetly checked the school roster. Mickey Molloy had attended the same year as Paddy Connolly. Two down, two to go.

Evelyn shook her head. "And that time Mickey's son Peter, no more than seven, drew a picture of his family with a blond lass. When I questioned who she was, he said it was his father's girlfriend. The things children say."

Hmm. Maybe Peter grew up thinking it was normal to have a girlfriend on the side. Like father, like son? If Finn's dad was a womanizer, he might not even recall Finn's mom. Maybe he'd had copies of that family photo and had given them to dozens of women. But why, if he hadn't wanted to be found?

She set the photo on the table and took a bite of lemon bread. "My, this is lovely. You must give me the recipe."

"I didn't make it, but thank you."

Evelyn veered off topic, complaining about last night's winner on the popular gameshow *Tipping Point* and the outrageous cost of property taxes—six grand less a year than you'd pay on a tiny ranch house in the States. Property taxes would be one of the only things I could afford on Grandma's house.

Evelyn returned to the photo while sipping her tea. "Not sure, but I'd say that's Tommy Lynch. Those lads were always together. As well as Alexander O'Donnell."

I checked the roster. Tommy wasn't listed the year the other two first appeared, but he'd attended the following year along with Alexander. Score!

"Tommy was a much-better-behaved student than a parent. His children could do no wrong. Although I shouldn't blame him as much as that wife of his...Gretta."

Grumpy Gretta? My stomach clenched.

"Well, I'll be looking for a reunion invite from Maggie before long. Usually comes in the post early spring so people can mark it on their calendars."

"My grandma actually just passed away."

The woman gave my hand a sympathetic squeeze. "I'm so sorry. What a lovely woman she was." Her gazed narrowed with curiosity. "Does this mean there'll be no more reunions?"

"Ah, I'm hoping to still have one in June."

Her frown turned into a smile.

While reminiscing about the last reunion, Evelyn's eyelids grew heavy and her head dropped back against the chair.

Biddy's eyes widened. "Janey Mac! Didn't just die, did she?"

"You're the nurse."

Biddy didn't have to check for a pulse since the woman started snoring. We covered her with a colorfully knitted afghan and wrote a thank-note for the wonderful visit.

Walking to the car, I asked Biddy, "Is Tommy Lynch's wife Grumpy Gretta, the mean daffodil lady?"

Biddy cringed. "That's her."

My palms started sweating.

When Biddy and I were eight, we wanted to surprise my

grandma and Biddy's mom with flowers. A quarter mile up from Biddy's was a long stretch of yellow daffodils lining both sides of the road. Assuming they were wildflowers, we yanked them out by their roots and piled them in Biddy's wagon. The wagon bounced along the pothole-filled road, daffodils flying out, leaving a trail of evidence. After we snipped off all the roots, we filled every one of Grandma's vases and empty bottles with the flowers. Once we ran out of containers, we planted the remaining ones in two pots on the front stoop. We'd had no clue they wouldn't grow without roots.

Upon finding her daffodils gone, Gretta Lynch hopped in her car and sped around the countryside searching for the flower thief. The trail of daffodils on the road led her right to us. She spied the potted flowers on Grandma's stoop and flew out of her car like a crazy woman as Grandma was pulling into the drive. Gretta accused us of stealing her daffodils, which we innocently denied, still thinking the common flowers grew in the wild. The horrible woman yanked a handful of the perky flowers from the soil. Biddy and I'd burst into tears over her ruining our gift. Grandma defended us, insisting it was an honest mistake. Gretta flipped out, threatening to file charges unless we replaced the flowers. That fall, Grandma, Biddy, and her mom planted a hundred daffodil bulbs along Gretta's road.

I grimaced. "I sure hope one of the Lynch boys doesn't turn out to be Finn's father."

"No kidding." Biddy hopped into the driver's seat, and I gladly handed her the keys. "They have two boys. Ian farms, and Rory works in Navan. Their oldest son died years ago while visiting the States. Don't recall his name. My dad's good friends with Alexander O'Donnell's son Jamie. Hangs around the pub a lot. I went to school with his daughter Anna. Same age as me, so Jamie would have been married at the time Finn was born. Has a single brother still living in the area. Even if it turns out Jamie is Finn's father, they both have a right to know."

"Agreed. Does Mickey Molloy have sons?"

"Three. Mattie lives nearby. I believe Peter's in Dublin and David's in England."

"Was he in England in 1990?"

"Haven't a clue. Might be easier if we discreetly pluck a piece of hair from a member of each family and run a DNA test."

"That's not how it works. You have to spit in a vial."

Yet it might still be easier to collect spit when the only clue we had to go on was Finn's father had visited Liverpool on January 8, 1990. Now having identified the four boys, our search would surely gain momentum.

Forward momentum, hopefully.

Eight

WE PULLED into my grandma's drive just minutes before the septic man arrived in a large truck with a blue hose wrapped around a red tank on the back. He accessed the tank in the middle of the half-acre backyard through a side gate. Biddy and I went into the house to nervously await the outcome.

"That smell is horrendous." I closed the living room window, having opened it minutes earlier to air out the dampness.

"Did ya expect it to smell like roses?"

"No. I just didn't realize I'd smell it all the way inside the house. And it's not exactly a quiet process." I sprayed lavender air freshener around the room.

Biddy waved a hand through the air. "Enough. Anymore lavender and we'll sleep for days."

I plopped down on the couch. "If it costs more than my credit card limit, I'm screwed."

"If it does, I'll help ya out. You'll be getting money from the sale."

"The costs of being a homeowner are insane. Septic tank, chimney, and boiler maintenance, which doesn't even include the petrol and peat to operate them. And don't even get me started on how expensive fuel is here. Then when something major needs replacing, like a septic system, how can a single person afford it? Frosted Flakes cost twice as much here as in the US."

"Buy Tesco's brand. If a rellie was leaving me a house, I wouldn't be whining about it. I'd be fixing it. And I'd be living on Tesco's ginger biscuits if I had to."

"You also have a full-time reliable job with a steady income."

"You would too if you lived here."

"I change jobs seasonally. Who'd hire me with that track record?"

"With your background you could work at a B & B, walk sheep..."

"Me, walking sheep? Seriously? Besides, I don't think there's a big demand here for a sheep walker. But that's another thing. I'd have to be walking everywhere. I couldn't afford a house in addition to car taxes and insurance."

"Owning a car is cheaper than paying for rentals every time you visit." She collapsed back in the chair. "I'm wrecked just listening to your complaining."

The noise outside stopped. I peeked out the window. The guy gave me the thumbs-up to test the toilet. I flew into the bathroom and flushed it. A water funnel swirled down, off to the septic tank. Yay. I still had a savings account. I met the man out front and paid him cash.

"Should be grand for another year. Just don't be letting it get to that point before emptying."

I nodded. "Won't be my responsibility next year."

The realization that this was my final stay at Grandma's hit me like a concrete tank. My excitement about not having to fork over thousands of euros to fix the system faded. Then a sense of pride rose inside me that I'd just successfully handled my first domestic challenge.

My emotions were all over the place.

Biddy invited me to dinner, so I grabbed a pan of lasagna and we headed up to the pub. Her parents could likely fill in more info for the four families we'd identified in Finn's photo.

"That's Jamie's car." Biddy gestured to a gray sedan in front of McCarthy's pub. "This is our lucky day. We can get answers from Jamie firsthand."

"So how should we approach the subject?"

"His mum was English, so they often visited rellies there. His daughter Anna and her mum once took a train into London to shop at Harrods." Biddy gave her eyes an exaggerated roll. "Never heard the bloody end of that story."

Inside the pub three young guys were playing darts and a familiar-looking man sat at the bar, chatting with Biddy's dad. She introduced me to Jamie. His blue eyes weren't nearly as bright as Finn's, but he had the same dark hair except for graying at the temples. And the two men were about the same height. Hmm...

"Ah, Maggie Flanagan's granddaughter, are ya?" he said. "Was sorry to hear about her passing. A fine woman, she was. Did a wonderful job maintaining the integrity of the old schoolhouse. Hope the future owners do the same. Heard ya had an offer on the place."

Who hadn't heard about the offer? Which reminded me —I still hadn't heard from the agent.

I nodded. "I'll make sure of it.

"How's the craic?" he asked Biddy. "Haven't seen ya in a while."

"Work's been brutal. I'll be needing a hollie soon. We were just talking about hopping over to England for a long weekend. You have rellies there, don't ya?"

Jamie nodded. "My mum grew up outside Manchester."

"Near Liverpool, isn't it?"

"Not far."

Man, she was smooth.

"Been thinking on visiting Liverpool," she said. "You ever been there?"

"Several times. Not in a while though. It's grand."

Biddy looked ready to burst with excitement and announce that Jamie had a son. "Mags's granny had a snap of your dad. Thought you might be liking a copy."

I slipped the picture from my purse and handed it to Jamie.

He studied the photo. "Which lad ya be thinking is my father?"

I pointed out the boy Evelyn had identified as Alexander O'Donnell.

Jamie shook his head. "My dad was a blond lad and not nearly that trim."

Biddy's dad peered over the bar at the photo. "I'd say he's not your dad. He's mine."

Biddy's smile vanished. "That's gramps? Are ya sure?"

Luckily both men were focused on the photo rather than her shocked reaction.

So much for Finn looking like Jamie. He bore a faint resemblance to Biddy's dad in both height and build. Daniel's eyes weren't as blue as the Aegean Sea, but... Holy cats. Earlier, I'd compared Finn's eyes to Biddy's parents' anniversary cruise.

Her dad nodded. "My mum had the snap in a scrapbook."

Was it *still* in the scrapbook, or had he given it to Finn's mom thirty years ago?

Biddy's dad had two sisters, no brothers. If Finn was a McCarthy, Daniel had to be his father. Oh boy. Biddy's parents had been married at the time Finn was born.

Biddy's phone rang, and she jumped, on edge. After a brief conversation, she peered over at me. "That was my friend Nellie at work. Finn's awake."

A sense of relief washed over me. Hopefully, Finn remembered the accident and the time leading up to it. If he confirmed someone ran him off the road, I could tell the garda officer I told you so and to start assisting me with the investigation.

"Who's Finn?" her dad asked.

Possibly your son.

"The fella in the bad car accident the other day," I said.

"Ah, right. The one who'd stopped at your place hoping to find his father?"

I nodded. Thankfully, I'd been so shaken up about Finn's accident that I hadn't shown Daniel the picture.

I peered over at Biddy. "Let's go see him before visiting hours are over."

As soon as we were out the door, Biddy said, "No way is my dad Finn's father. He never would have cheated on my mum. And he didn't look the least bit freaked out by the photo."

I hadn't noticed his reaction since I'd been watching Biddy's. However, he had looked a bit reminiscent when mentioning he hadn't seen the photo in years.

"Didn't your mom go live with her sister for six months when we were seven? And your parents went to marriage counseling?"

"A lot of couples go to counseling. I'm not accusing my father of cheating when we have no evidence." She marched across the road toward the car. "We'll figure out which of the *other* boys in the snap is Finn's grandfather, so we won't even need to consider my dad."

"What if we can't confirm one of the other boys is Finn's grandpa? What if it turns out—"

"It won't. And if it does...we aren't telling Finn."

"That's not fair."

Biddy glared at me. "Ruining my parents' marriage isn't fair either."

"I wouldn't want to break up their marriage, but what happened to Finn having the right to know his father even if it'd been Jamie, who's married?"

"That was before it might have been *my* father."

"It happened thirty-one years ago. Your parents would undoubtedly work through it. And it might turn out you'd have a brother and a sibling you like."

Biddy made a detour toward their residence around back of the pub. "Let's put this to rest right now. If the snap's in our family album, that rules out my dad."

"And if it's not?"

She shook her head and flew into the house. We skidded

to a halt upon encountering her mom, Ita, grabbing a bottled water from the fridge. Dressed in teal yoga pants and a pink top, her blond hair was styled in a chin-length bob. Being a hairdresser, she changed her style as often as I changed jobs.

"You girls are just in time for dinner. What should we have?"

I set the aluminum pan on the counter. "How about lasagna?"

"Ah, what a luv ya are. Thanks a mil."

"We just need to run into the hospital and see how the fella from the accident's faring," Biddy said.

Ita frowned. "Hope he's in good form. Well, at least as good as can be expected." She shook her head. "His poor parents. I'd go mad if you were in a near-fatal car crash." She glanced over at me. "Either of you." Eyes watering, she swooped in for a group hug.

Would she be that supportive if Finn turned out to be her stepson?

She released her embrace. "I'll leave some of the lasagna for when you get back."

I smiled. "Thanks. I'll bring up a few more dishes."

"Would be lovely not having to cook a few nights."

Excellent. Two down and fourteen to go.

Biddy headed toward the living room. "Just going to take a quick look at the photo albums. Wanted to show Mags a snap."

"The albums aren't here. Your aunt Marie has them down in Cork."

Biddy spun around toward her mom. "Why does she have them in Cork?"

Ita looked surprised by Biddy's harsh tone. "Because

that's where she lives. She wanted to scan copies of the photos."

Biddy looked ready to stomp her foot in a hissy fit. "When is she returning them?"

Ita shrugged. "Next time she visits, I'd suppose. What snap's so important you have to show Mags now?"

Biddy shook her head in frustration. "Never mind." She marched out the door.

I shared Ita's confused look and flew out the door. Biddy was already to the car by the time I caught up with her. She hopped inside and slammed the door. I joined her.

"Gee, that wasn't the least bit suspicious," I said. "If you're going to be helping me, you need to work on your poker face and sleuthing skills. What if your mom mentions to your dad that you just came unglued over some photo? He'll know which one and wonder why."

"My auntie Marie won't be up to visit for months."

"Email her the photo and ask if the original is in the album or you'll get a copy from me. Why would your dad have admitted to ever having the pic if he'd given it away?"

Biddy scratched her neck. "Doesn't matter. We're going to figure out which of the *other* families is Finn's."

"But your aunt could easily resolve the matter if—"

"Drop it." Biddy's stern tone reminded me of the time she'd told me to drop the last piece of confetti cake at her ninth birthday party.

She was obviously afraid to know the truth.

"I certainly hope Evelyn McCreery was right about the other two boys being Mickey Molloy and Tommy Lynch. I don't want any more surprises." Although I couldn't imagine a bigger one than Biddy's dad.

If Daniel McCarthy turned out to be Finn's father, they both had the right to know the truth. I was more concerned that someone in Biddy's family might have tried to kill Finn. What if Finn had been showing the pic around McCarthy's pub the night Biddy's mom had been bartending? No way had Ita come unhinged and run Finn off the road without proof he was her husband's illegitimate child. Even with proof, she wouldn't have done it.

Biddy's sister, Clare, was another story. She'd once snapped the head off Biddy's Barbie doll and whipped her Tickle Me Elmo against the wall in anger. Besides losing an eye, Elmo couldn't stop giggling, sounding like he'd gone completely mad.

Clare hated the pub business but would flip out if she had to share the profits with Finn in addition to Biddy. If Clare weren't visiting her husband's family in Belfast, she'd be at the top of my list with Stella.

Nine

Biddy scratched at her red neck, staring at the closed door to Finn's hospital room.

I slapped away her hand. "You don't have to come in. Wait out here for me."

She took a deep breath. "No, I want to see how he's doing."

Inside the room, Finn was sitting up in bed, drinking a glass of water. I returned his smile, whereas Biddy merely stared.

"My dad's eyes aren't nearly that blue," she muttered.

Yet they were blue, and he was tall and broad shouldered like Finn.

I introduced Biddy as my friend rather than as his possible sibling.

"You were here yesterday, right?" he asked me. "It wasn't a dream?"

I stifled a grin at the thought of Finn dreaming about me. What was that about?

"No, you weren't dreaming."

"I told you someone ran me off the road?"

"Not exactly. You warned me to be careful. But I thought that might have been what you meant. You need to tell the garda. They wouldn't believe me, even though the eyewitness left the scene rather than calling 999. Do you remember anything? The color of the car?"

"It's a blur. Except I'm sure it was intentional."

I slipped Finn's note from my purse and handed it to him. "Yesterday when I visited, the nurse gave me this message you'd written. Be careful... Little Red Riding Hood. Does that mean anything to you?"

Finn stared at the note, shaking his head.

"Could you have been referring to the car behind you? The police didn't confirm it, but I believe the eyewitness drove a red car."

He dropped his head back against the bed in frustration.

"It's okay." I smiled like everything was super. "Don't push it. I bet you meant the red car."

He nodded faintly, his shoulders relaxing.

"I have good news. We've identified the boys in the photo."

Best to wait until he was on the mend to tell him his photo was likely stolen by the person who'd run him off the road. He'd be devastated if he hadn't made copies. At least I had a copy on my phone.

"Actually, *three* of the *four* boys have been identified." Biddy shot me a cautious look. "And we need to reconfirm two of them but are fairly certain they're correct."

Finn perked up. "That's grand. Are they still alive? Living in the area?"

I nodded. "All but one of the three known boys are alive.

Need to verify their sons."

"What are their names?"

"Last names are Molloy, Lynch, and Connolly." If I provided first names, I was afraid Finn would leave the hospital to find them. He was safer here than out on the road.

The corners of his mouth curled into an intrigued smile. "Molloy, Lynch, Connolly..." He peered over at Biddy. "You're local. Do you know the families? Any of them I wouldn't want to be belonging to?"

Biddy was undoubtedly thinking *hers*, but she said, "All good families."

Finn's smile faded. "I appreciate your help, and this information is brilliant, but I'm not sure you should continue. Look at what happened to me. I don't want you getting hurt over this. I'd been hesitant to search for my father. Thought if he'd changed his mind about seeing my mum again, he likely wouldn't be keen on meeting me. And then this happened."

"Stay positive," I said. "Don't think the worst, that your father did this. Do you remember who you talked to right before the accident?"

He shook his head, gazing out the window at the dark sky threatening rain. "He fancied the Beatles."

"Someone in a pub?"

"My father. My mum met him in a pub where a Beatles tribute band was playing. I've been there several times. A small hole-in-the-wall place down an alley. Before that band was a trad music session. He mentioned playing the fiddle."

Biddy's dad sometimes played the fiddle when he'd had too many pints. Not very well, but he played it.

"Once I knew he was a Beatles fan, I acquired the group's entire album collection and saw Paul McCartney in concert twice. As if I might run into my father there."

I nodded enthusiastically. "These are great clues."

"He drank Keegans whiskey, which isn't real common, and neither is being allergic to cats. When leaving the pub, they came across one. My mum loves cats, but he asked her not to pet the yoke due to his allergies."

A sense of optimism rose inside me. Once we learned the three men's sons, these clues would help us determine Finn's dad. How difficult could it be to find a fiddle-playing Irish Beatles' fan who drank Keegans whiskey and was allergic to cats?

Biddy smiled. "My dad's not allergic to cats."

Finn gave her a curious look, while I shot her a cautious one.

She shrugged it off. "Talking about dads and allergies made me think of mine."

"My mum wondered if that was the case or if he merely didn't fancy cats," he said.

Biddy's smile faded. When we were twelve, we'd found a kitten while bicycling down their road. Her father wouldn't allow her to keep it, not liking cats. Beatrice had ended up living with Grandma for nine years.

"Did your mom ever mention if you look like your father?" I asked.

He shook his head. "But I must have gotten my height from him. She's short with dark hair and green eyes. She can't carry a tune or play an instrument. When I learned he played the fiddle, I gave it a go. I did okay at it but prefer the guitar."

"Sounds like you inherited his musical talent."

"I'm definitely more the creative type than my mum, who can calculate math in her head. I do the marketing for our family's woolen company."

I had no clue what I'd inherited from my biological father. Maybe his sense of optimism and adventure, since I certainly hadn't gotten those traits from my mother.

"She was the bookkeeper before moving to Savannah."

I smiled. "My dad lives just a few hours south in Jacksonville."

"Haven't made it to Florida yet. I visit Savannah at least once a year but avoid summers. They're brutal."

"Your mum has never taken you to see Mickey and Minnie?" Biddy asked.

"No, she's not much for crowds."

"Well, I've been inviting myself to someone's house in Florida for years, wanting to visit Epcot Center, but the person can't seem to take a hint." She slid me a sideways gaze.

"My father has only lived there *three* years, and the last time you invited yourself was during Hurricane Irma."

"As if I'm not used to a bit of rain and gale-force winds," she said.

I rolled my eyes and peered over at Finn. "When do you think you'll be released?"

"In a few days. Not sure if I'll head back to Wexford for a bit to mend or stay in the area."

"You can crash at my place until you're feeling better." My heart raced. I couldn't believe I'd just blurted that out. Neither could Biddy, who stood there gaping at me.

"I wouldn't want to be putting you in more danger by

moving in with ya. Our being *engaged* is putting you in enough." He quirked a sly smile.

Heat exploded on my cheeks; my gaze darted to Biddy.

"Yeah, I was the one who told the nurses that so they'd let Mags in for a visit."

"Ah, right, then. I assumed there was a logical explanation."

"Okay, get some rest. We'll see you again soon." I bolted for the door even though it was my body on fire and not the building. Zipping past the nurses' station, I smiled at my new friend and snatched a few chocolates from the candy bowl.

Biddy power-walked next to me down the hall. "I can't believe you offered to play nursemaid to Finn."

"I'm not the nurse—you are." I unwrapped the chocolate and popped it into my mouth.

"Excuse me?"

"If he starts taking a turn for the worse, you're just up the road. I thought that would make it an ideal spot for him." I hadn't given *any* thought to the reasons Finn should stay with me when I'd blurted out the offer. "Finn confirmed it wasn't an accident. Someone is after him."

"If someone is trying to stop him from learning his father's identity, the person will now likely try to stop you. And me. But this is my town and Finn might be..."

Her brother?

A determined look hardened Biddy's features. "I'm not having a murderer on the loose. Or rather a wannabe murderer. A wannabe murderer is even worse than a proper murderer. The person is apt to get sloppy and hurt innocent people. Might be running my father or Edmond off the road. We don't want to be responsible for either of their deaths."

As convoluted as her reasoning was, I agreed.

We had to protect Ballycaffey. There was no room there for an improper or proper killer. And it was up to us to stop the person. Now knowing more than the date and location Finn was conceived bolstered our confidence.

Hopefully, it wasn't *false* confidence.

I pulled off on the side of the road, across from McCarthy's pub. "What was I thinking telling Finn he could stay with me?" I was in full-blown panic mode. Like time to start breathing into a paper bag panic mode. "I haven't had a relationship since Josh. Not that this is a relationship, but I need to date a guy before moving in with one. I didn't even live with Josh."

"Because you guys were never together in the same town for more than a few days."

True. In the six months we'd dated, we'd maybe spent thirty days together. He was a freelance nature photographer. We both loved to travel, but our marriage never would have lasted if we hadn't traveled together.

"What was I thinking?" I let out a frustrated moan.

"About Josh or Finn?"

"Finn."

"I haven't a clue. About either of them actually."

"What if *he's* thinking there's more to my offer than Irish hospitality?"

"Not like you're going to be sharing a bedroom. Sleep downstairs in your granny's room."

My top lip curled back. "She was laid out in her bed for

the wake. I'm not sleeping in it. Maybe he could stay with you."

Biddy's eyes widened. "Mad, are ya?"

"Tell your parents you're picking up a side job as an in-home caregiver."

"I'd be doing it in *his* home if that was the case."

"What if—"

"You'd kept your gob shut and not made the offer?"

"What if he *is* your brother?"

Biddy smacked my arm. "Stop saying that." She stepped from the car and slammed the door.

We entered the pub, where Biddy's dad and several older men were engrossed in a dart tournament on TV. Five minutes of watching darts, I was ready to poke my eye out with one.

Biddy's mom breezed into the bar from their residence dressed in magenta-colored yoga pants and a black top. She gave her husband a kiss, then joined us.

"Did ya know these two lassies here are planning a trip to England?" Daniel asked his wife.

"Hadn't a clue. When did ya be deciding this?"

"We could use a hollie about now," Biddy said.

Her mom looked like we were nuts. "England in the dead of winter? Why not Portugal or Lanzarote?"

"I've been to both a dozen times," Biddy whined.

One summer I'd joined Biddy's family on a week's holiday to the Canary Islands, off the coast of Africa. Being from Chicago, my fair skin had never been exposed to the broiling sun nearer the equator. When I turned fifty and a dermatologist diagnosed me with skin cancer, I'd be able to trace it back to a wicked sunburn that trip.

"Have either of you been to Liverpool?" I clamped my teeth down on my lower lip, but it was too late.

Biddy's glare about singed off the rest of my left eyebrow.

A group of rowdy men entered the pub. Daniel gave them a wave and grabbed a Guinness glass.

Ita shook her head. "Never been there." She left to reheat our lasagna.

Biddy swiveled toward me on her stool. "What happened to proving one of the other three families is Finn's and leaving mine out of it for now? What if my dad did have an affair in Liverpool and my mom knew about it?"

"Then he's Finn's father."

"You know what I mean. Don't go dredging up the past if we don't have to."

"Sorry. It just slipped out. But if we can rule out your dad, he'd be a great resource."

"I'm a great resource. I've already given you loads of info. And anything I don't know I can discreetly find out." Biddy's gaze narrowed on a poster behind the bar advertising the Drumcara tractor run. "Some of the potential fathers will be in the run this weekend. We could offer to help with soup and sandwiches. Would give us an excuse to be mingling with everyone. Could put a cat in one of them baby slings and carry it around to see if anyone has a sneezing fit."

"Oh yeah, that wouldn't make us look the least bit suspicious."

"My sister's a horrible housekeeper. There'd be loads of cat fur under her couch. I can vacuum up a bag when I'm over there feeding Blarney. We could stuff it in our pockets."

I nodded. "That might work."

"I'll recognize most except for maybe Rory Lynch. If he

works in Navan and doesn't farm, he mightn't be doing the run anyway."

"I met the bartender at the Drumcara pub. Had a nice conversation. I could pop over in the morning and offer to help out."

"After that we can call in on one or two of the families before I have to work. Can ask questions for the reunion roster and offer them a copy of the snap. Might get enough info from the parents that we can narrow it down to the right son."

"We should visit Rosie again now that we have more clues about Finn's father and try to learn if Sean was for sure adopted." Seeing as Evelyn McCreery had identified Biddy's grandpa as Alexander O'Donnell, she might have been wrong about the adoption. "Maybe Edmond can visit Gretta and Tommy Lynch. Having helped my grandma with past reunions will give him some credibility for nosing around."

"Ah, shame on ya. Can't be feeding that poor man to the wolves all by himself. You need to be going with him."

"Why do I have to visit Grumpy Gretta?"

"Because I've seen her plenty since the daffodil disaster. And I visited Rosie after desecrating her parents' graves."

"Fine. Edmond and I'll go visit the Lynches. Maybe she won't remember me."

"Are you kidding? That woman remembers every daffodil she's ever planted or that *I've* planted. She'll remember ya."

"Thanks for the pep talk. Then you and I'll visit the Molloys. Have we ever done anything to upset them? Just want to make sure I'm prepared."

Biddy shook her head. "Not that I know of."

I had a feeling that was about to change.

Ten

THE FOLLOWING MORNING, a young girl rather than Stella was working at the Drumcara convenience store. Good thing or I might have confronted the liar about having seen the newspaper clipping at her sweet mother-in-law's, Rosie's. And that she had better fess up about her plans to sell the Connollys' land. However, Stella had better not be at the hospital visiting Finn. According to Biddy, the nurse at the reception desk on Finn's floor confirmed his blond visitor hadn't returned. Yet she hadn't a clue that Stella had been there the *first* time. The woman wasn't exactly a reliable source.

I headed inside O'Sullivan's pub to volunteer Biddy and my services for the tractor run.

George greeted me with a welcoming smile. "Well, hello there, lassie."

I eyed the large tongue graphic plastered on his Rolling Stone's T-shirt. "'Honky Tonk Women' is a great dance tune. So is 'Start Me Up.'"

George clapped. "Very impressive. Makes up for ya thinking Phil Lynott was a hurler."

"The Stones are my dad's favorite band. He has all their albums."

"Actual vinyl?"

"Of course." I slid up onto a barstool.

"That's brilliant. My brother Brody and I saw them in concert at Slane Castle back in 2007. Great craic." Thoughts of partying at a Stones concert put a grin on his face.

"My dad was a regular groupie. Saw them three times on their 1981 tour. I'd been happy to see Justin Timberlake once. My dad took my friend and me. My mom had a fit because she thought 'SexyBack' was not the kind of song a thirteen-year-old girl should be dancing to."

He laughed. "Is your mum or dad Irish?"

"My mom. But my dad bought me an airline ticket to Ireland for my first solo flight when I was fifteen. My mom went berserk." Mom had always been quick to judge my dad, everyone actually, and then look at what she did to my dad and me. A bit hypocritical. "But I won't get into my family drama." I nodded at the poster advertising the tractor run behind the bar. "I saw the sign outside. I'd be happy to donate soup or sandwiches." Or how about a shepherd's pie? I still had fourteen meals to give away. "My friend Biddy McCarthy has helped her dad with runs and wanted to make the offer. It's for such a great cause."

"I'd certainly never turn away volunteers. Sandwiches would be grand."

"How many tractors are signed up, so we have an idea on the number to make?"

"A hundred and three so far. However, there's always some drop off."

Holy cats! That would clean out my savings. Biddy and I'd have to haul our butts out of bed at 2:00 a.m. to start making sandwiches. Panic apparently reflected on my face.

George smiled. "Two others are also bringing sandwiches. Twenty-five should be plenty, cut in quarters."

I breathed a relieved sigh. "Sounds good. If Biddy's neighbors haven't all signed up, she'd be happy to recruit them."

"Not sure who all registered." He handed me a binder from behind the bar. "Take a look if you'd like."

I'd like very much.

I paged through the registrant list, including Mattie Molloy and Ian Lynch. We'd have to figure out a way to track down the other five men, especially since I couldn't afford a road trip to England to meet one of them.

Aileen and Mickey Molloy lived in an impressive Georgian-style home with several outbuildings set back from the road.

"If their home is any indication, the Molloys likely own a fair share of the surrounding farmland," I told Biddy. "Would one of the sons not want the farm shared with Finn? Not want him building a house on their family land? Remember, this is the only family we haven't ticked off at some point in our lives, and now's not the time to change that." I stepped from the car and set the pan of Irish stew on the roof while I stripped off my fleece jacket. With the sun now out, it was nearing fifty.

"Ah, that's absolutely brilliant." Biddy laughed at my green sweatshirt that read *Bluffy McLiarpants* with four playing cards, all aces.

"Got it when I was working that casino cruise in New Orleans. Thought it was a wee bit Irish."

"That it is."

The three-hour cruise had been on board an old-fashioned paddleboat. I'd worn an emerald-green satin dress with frilly layers and a corset top that laced up the back. If I'd been in France, I'd have been a can-can dancer rather than a saloon girl. I'd greeted boarding passengers with business cards and corny lines, such as, "I must say, sir, you do look like a gambling man to me." Trying to entice men to dress up in one of the many period riverboat gambler costumes for a vintage photoshoot. If a woman looked more like a southern-belle type than a saloon girl, I'd do my Scarlett O'Hara impersonation. "Ma'am, I do declare, you're as pretty as a peach, and I have the most delightful dress for you." It'd been loads of fun except for having to starve myself for four months to fit in the dress.

A woman with short gray hair in green wellies, faded jeans, and a men's flannel jacket waved from a fenced-in area. A half dozen baby goats in colorful knitted sweaters frolicked around her. It was a social media video waiting to go viral.

"Hello there," Aileen said. "Come on back. You're just in time to help me feed the lads."

"Cute little fellas, aren't they?" Biddy said.

I nodded. They were cute and little. Nothing like that huge mean sheep with the crazed look in its eyes that chased me up the road. Or the one camped out in my yard.

"They're fenced in. Can't be chasing ya nowhere.

Aileen's pride and joy. Has raised them for years." Biddy turned to me and lowered her voice. "Are you okay?"

"I'm fine." I set the pan of stew on a picnic table. I opened the gate and entered the fenced-in area.

"Be sure to watch where you're walking," Aileen said.

I didn't have to ask why. The scent of wet earth mingled with the smell of goat poop.

A goat in a green sweater hopped sideways toward me. I hopped back up against the fence. It nuzzled my leg.

Aileen smiled. "Ah, already taken to ya, he has. Being bottle-fed, they're quite friendly yokes." She handed me a glass bottle filled with milk.

"I've never fed a goat."

"You'll be grand. Kneel down, and he'll come right up and start feeding from the bottle."

I knelt. The goat trotted toward me. I instinctively pressed my hands out in front of me. The goat jumped at the bottle in my hand. Aileen lowered my hand, allowing the animal easier access. It began sucking on the nipple.

"Ah, fair play to ya." Aileen gave me a reassuring pat on the shoulder. "Keep talking to the little fella and looking him in the eyes. Makes 'em trust ya."

Believe me, I wasn't taking my eyes off this goat for a second and giving it the edge.

Biddy looked like a pro feeding one in a red sweater. "Mickey still playing the fiddle?"

"That he is. Of course, not as much with the lads now that they're grown. Not sure if David is playing at all. Living in England, we don't see much of him and his partner. Thinks we don't approve of his lifestyle, but that's just an excuse not to visit. Both Mickey and I think Ethan is a fine fella."

Cross David off the list of possible fathers.

"Funny, Mattie studied a year in Manchester, so we always figured he'd be the one to live there. Instead he became disenchanted with city life and returned home to farm."

"When was that?" I asked. "I'd like to add the boys' ages and any interesting facts to the reunion rosters."

If I could remember it all without taking notes.

"In the early nineties. Don't recall the precise year. I could ask him if you'd like."

"That's close enough."

"Nice to have two sons still playing, anyway," Biddy said.

"'Tis lovely, except makes it a wee bit difficult who to leave the family fiddle to. Mickey's dad was a bit of a celebrity, ya know. Played with the Limerick Lads. Left Mickey his instrument."

Just how valuable was that fiddle? Worth running Finn off the road over?

"When you rang, I was glad to hear there'll be a school reunion this summer. It's lovely that you're continuing the tradition. Your grandma would be so proud of you."

"I thought it best, in her memory."

"So glad the rumor that you're selling the place wasn't true."

"Well, actually it is."

Aileen's smile faded. "How can you be holding the reunion there if you don't own the place?"

"It'll be at McCarthy's pub. We'll have the annual photo take in front of the house."

"Mickey and I shared our first kiss behind the schoolhouse. We were ten." The memory brought a smile to her lips, a sparkle to her eyes. "Can you believe that? I only kissed one other boy after that. I knew Mickey was the one. Every reunion we kiss under the large ash tree, just like sixty years ago."

One more thing to add to the sales agreement—preserve the ash tree.

"Same tree our Mattie fell from and broke his wrist. He blamed mischievous fairies, seeing as he wasn't supposed to be climbing the tree. Fair play to him at only nine knowing a fairy tree was hawthorn or ash."

The new owners also needed to care for the fairies!

Grandma and I once made a fairy garden under the ash tree. Sadly, gale-force winds had wiped it out before I'd returned for another visit.

I slipped Finn's photo from my back jeans pocket and handed it to Aileen. "My grandma had this. I thought it would be nice to display at the reunion. Would you like a copy?"

"I most certainly would. Mickey will be over the moon. We searched high and low for this snap years ago and couldn't find it. I went through every box and drawer in the house."

Biddy and I exchanged curious glances over the missing photo.

Done eating, my goat scampered off to play.

A sense of pride rose inside me over having been in such close contact with the animal. A step toward overcoming my fear of sheep. I stood and realized I was missing an earring. The ones Grandma had given me for Christmas this year.

Hoping it had just fallen out, I dropped down on all fours, frantically searching the ground. I peered up as a blue-sweatered goat sprang into the air, his hooves landing on my back with a thud, knocking the wind out of me. He leaped off.

"What...the..." I gasped for air. "...what..."

Biddy rushed over. "Stay calm. Don't be upsetting Aileen." She offered me her hand, peering over at the woman. "Ah, she's grand."

"Am...not." I pushed up onto my knees. I rolled my shoulders, making sure they still worked. Pain radiated from my right one, where a hoof had dug under my shoulder blade.

So much for overcoming my fear of sheep.

Aileen and Biddy each took a hand, helping me stand.

"Sorry about that," Aileen said. "Are ya okay?"

"She's grand," Biddy said. "Aren't ya?"

I nodded faintly.

"He's just learned that trick, but usually it's off one of his mates. He must really have taken to ya, thinking you're one of the family now. How lovely is that?"

Not lovely at all.

I sat on a bench outside the pen trying to recover while Biddy searched for my earring.

A gray truck pulled up the drive.

"Ah, Mickey's home." Aileen gave her husband a wave and went over to greet him.

Biddy returned with my earring, undamaged except for the missing back. I slipped it into my jeans pocket. From now on the earrings were only for special occasions.

I turned my back toward Biddy. "Check and see if I'm bleeding or if anything is broken."

"I'm not going to be looking at your back and upsetting poor Aileen by making her think you're hurt."

"I *am* hurt."

"Would be rude for you to say so."

"It's rude for her goat to break a guest's back."

"You couldn't be walking if it were broken."

"Gee, thanks for the thorough diagnosis, Nurse Biddy."

"My mum has a chiropractor if you need one."

"I think I'll need a surgeon, but I can't afford either."

"I hate to tell ya, but poor Bluffy didn't fare well." She eyed the back of my sweatshirt. "His right shoulder is torn."

I growled. "That's where it dug its heel in under my shoulder blade. Do you think it can be repaired?"

"If you're referring to your shoulder blade, yes. Bluffy, no. He'll be playing poker and drinking pints with my uncle Seamus." She gazed off toward the sky. "He was quite good, so Bluffy be best to watch his back."

Bluffy certainly hadn't been watching *my* back.

Aileen and her husband headed toward us.

My eyes widened, but I snapped my mouth shut, catching a surprised gasp before it escaped. Mickey was the handsome older blue-eyed man I'd seen coming out of the Ballycaffey gas station the other day. The one who'd reminded me of Finn, except for his thick silver hair. He wore jeans and a light-gray sweater. He shook my hand, and a light fluttering tickled my chest. Granted, the man was quite charming and handsome for being more than twice my age, but what was with my reaction? Kind of like my reaction when I'd first met Finn...

What if Finn's father wasn't Mickey's *son* but Mickey *himself*? Had Finn's mom mentioned his father's age? Maybe she'd been attracted to an older man. Supposedly Mickey had been quite the charmer. One of his sons had drawn his father's girlfriend for art class.

The fact that I'd had such a strong reaction to Mickey before even knowing he was a possible father candidate had to be a sign, not merely a coincidence.

Aileen handed him the photo.

A twinkle sparkled in Mickey's blue eyes. "Wherever did you find that?"

"Maggie Flanagan had the snap. Her granddaughter here thought we might be liking a copy."

"We certainly would." Mickey smiled at the photo, a reminiscent look on his face. Was he thinking about Finn's mom? "This is my only photo with that little fella Charlie."

Or was the trip down memory lane over his dog Charlie?

Aileen gasped. "Oh, I should have mentioned Peter's coming from Dublin for the weekend. He and Mickey will be playing at Coffey's pub tonight." She glanced over at her husband. "We were just talking about our family of fiddlers."

"Aye, ya should come out. I'm a wee bit rusty. Not like when I toured with my father back twenty years ago."

"It was longer ago than that," Aileen said.

He nodded. "Suppose it was. Time goes so fast."

"Did you tour around Ireland?" I asked.

"And England."

Exactly what years was that?

"Sounds like great craic," Biddy said.

And an ideal opportunity to meet Peter from Dublin and

request a Beatles song. Maybe I could allow a stray cat to wander into the pub.

We thanked Aileen for her hospitality and promised Mickey we'd see him and his son at the pub tonight. As we headed toward the car, the goat in the green sweater stood at the fence, crying out.

"Ah, he misses ya already," Biddy said. "You'll have to call back in for a visit."

"Only if his brother in blue is tied up."

"Well, at least you handled it brilliantly so we can call back if needed. You didn't freak out and go flying out the pen, leaving the gate open for all the lads to escape and chase ya down the road to the pub." Biddy smirked.

"And you didn't fall into a grave."

She shrugged. "Fair play to us both."

"Their missing photo is a great clue."

Biddy went silent not wanting to discuss whether the snap was still in her family photo album at her aunt's down in Cork.

"We can rule out David," Biddy said.

"Unless that was a recent change of lifestyle."

"I'll ask my mum. We'll put him at the bottom of the list for now. And Mattie was in England in the early nineties."

"So was Mickey. He's quite handsome. Same bright-blue eyes as Finn. What if *he's* Finn's father? I'd never considered one of the boys in the photo until just meeting Mickey."

Biddy nodded. "True, he's good looking for an older fella. And the fact that Mickey's photo is missing cinches it. He has to be Finn's father."

"Is this you being unbiased?"

"It's me being right."

"We need to keep an open mind. Even about it having been Stella who ran Finn off the road. Mickey's sons have plenty of motives to not want an illegitimate brother around. Like the fiddle. A family heirloom worth who knows how much. All this farmland. And, of course, wanting to avoid the family drama."

As Biddy backed down the drive, we sniffed the air, which reeked like goat poop.

Biddy's top lip curled back. "What is that?"

We checked our shoes.

"Nothing but dirt and grass on mine," I said.

"Janey Mac!" Biddy whipped off her navy shoes and scraped them against the blacktop drive. She pulled wipes from the glove compartment and scrubbed the soles. "I have to be wearing these to work." She slipped her shoes back on.

I pulled up my sweatshirt for her to check out my back.

"Going to have a few bruises," she said. "No broken skin's good."

"What about broken bones?" I rotated my shoulder. "Its hoof dug under my right shoulder blade."

"Can't be broken with the way you're moving it."

Two guys drove past and lay on the horn, hooting and hollering at my raised shirt.

Biddy gave them a few unladylike gestures.

"As if they've never seen a girl without her shirt on," I said.

"Surely haven't. That was Jimmy and Lenny Walsh."

"Marjorie the Mouth's sons?"

Biddy nodded.

And my reputation just kept getting worse.

Eleven

恐	

WHEN BIDDY DROPPED me off at Grandma's, the pink sheep was lying on the blacktop drive sunning itself. My heart raced. My goat encounter had been a definite step backward in overcoming my fear of sheep. Yet I couldn't let this animal smell fear. Bluffy and I were in no condition to race up the road to McCarthy's pub and leap up on the bar. I looked the sheep straight in its beady black eyes, like I had the baby goat while feeding it. Rather than racing off, it held my gaze. According to Aileen, goats would run away from humans if they were afraid. And this sheep seemed quite sociable.

"Hey there, Pinky." Maybe it would warm to my cutesy name for it.

Pinky didn't flinch.

I maintained my distance, talking as I headed toward the door. I walked inside and peeked out the door window at the sheep still lying on the pavement, staring at me, curious what I was up to. Baby steps.

I entered the living room as a chill raced through me. I

banged a fist against the radiator, and pain crippled my right shoulder. The radiator let out a hiss. I hissed back. Out of peat again—was there a peat thief on the loose? I slipped on my wellies to head out to the shed.

The kitchen garbage can in the conservatory was half filled with water. Unable to lift it with my sore shoulder, I'd have to pan it out by hand later. En route to the woodshed, I made a detour over to the lone ash tree at the back of the yard. The fairy tree where Aileen and Mickey had shared their first kiss. I'd been so upset about the winds destroying my fairy garden, Grandma had suggested not replacing it. Gale-force winds were common in Ireland. The only surviving fairy-garden piece was a tiny weathered red door with yellow bees nailed to the base of the tree.

Hidden behind the door was a secret space for leaving the fairies notes, wishes, or gifts. The fairies' magical powers protected children from bad dreams and granted their wishes. With a bit of jiggling, the door opened, revealing a small clump of wet paper. The ink had washed out over the years, and the ball was mush.

I'd have to leave a new wish.

After hauling in peat, making a roaring fire, and turning on the three space heaters, I cracked open the windows. Crazy, yet even in the dead of winter everyone opened windows to dry out their houses and reduce the chance of mold. No mold was the one feature this house had going for it.

I exchanged my damaged sweatshirt for a blue wool sweater. The goat's hoof had ripped a three-inch tear in Bluffy. Grandma would have been able to sew or patch it, making it look good as new. Refusing to throw it away, I tossed it in the laundry hamper, pretending I'd repair it later.

An hour until I had to pick up Edmond for our visit with Gretta. Rather than getting drunk to ease my nerves, I plopped down on the couch with my laptop, needing a distraction. I moaned in pain upon my shoulder's impact with the cushion. I could feel each hoof mark on my back.

I needed to create family trees for Finn's possible fathers. Besides managing my DNA account, I knew my way around Ancestry.com and other research sites from years of assisting Grandma. Even if Finn's new DNA test results had a paternal second-cousin match, they'd share great-grandparents. So it was necessary to have the four men's family trees traced back at least that far to know any ancestors' surnames shared by Finn's top matches. That was dependent on Finn's matches providing trees back to *their* great-grandparents.

That was a big *if*.

I created a private tree for Mickey and Aileen Molloy and added my notes. Mattie farmed locally. Peter lived in Dublin, David in England. David was an unlikely candidate because of his life partner. Mickey's blue eyes reminded me of Finn's. Their photo had been missing for years. Family members were unlikely allergic to goats but unsure about cats. They all played the fiddle. Mickey had toured in England in the eighties and nineties. Mattie had studied in Manchester, near Liverpool.

I Googled Limerick Lads, finding info on Mickey's dad. Within minutes I'd located Dermot Molloy's obituary online along with articles about his contribution to Irish music. His obit provided the names of his parents, five siblings, and three children, including spouses. Dermot's wife's obit provided similar info for her side of the family. In fifteen minutes I'd traced the Molloys' paternal tree back to what might be Finn's two-time great-grandparents. A quick call to Edmond and I had Aileen *Weir* Molloy's parents' names and traced the boys' maternal line back to grandparents.

Tracing a family line back was often easier than tracing it forward. Not that it was usually as quick as the Molloys, but finding information on the living—Mickey's siblings and children—would require more sleuthing. Having every family member accounted for was critical since it was hard to say how Finn's DNA matches might be connected. My grandma had sometimes reached out to me for assistance with locating people's living relatives. Much of that research entailed perusing "people search" sites and social media pages, not her forte. She'd never even gotten the lingo correct. She'd phone me and say, "Can you check Tweeter to see if anyone has twitted about the person?"

Many people's social media pages weren't private. Even if they were, you could often view comments on certain posts. A person's Facebook friends list was a great resource but might not help you determine relationships. You could almost always find comments and tags such as *Thanks Auntie Marie* or *Happy Father's Day Uncle Jack*. Precisely why people in witness protection should steer clear of social media. There was no hiding on the web.

The Connollys' tree wouldn't take long, but I had to get ready to meet Edmond. If Sean was adopted, there was no need to trace his ancestors. If he wasn't, I now knew from Rosie's vacation photos that Paddy had some German ancestry on his mother's side.

The family I knew best, of course, was Biddy's. As much

as I'd like to, I couldn't rule out her dad. She'd have a fit if she knew I was creating her family tree.

I had to make sure she didn't find out.

On the way to Edmond's I made a quick stop at Grandma's childhood home, where her brother had lived before dying twenty-two years ago. Every few weeks she'd check to make sure the deserted dwelling was still standing and to clean up beer cans and litter. It was the ideal spot for a kids' party hangout, located down a one-lane road with few occupied homes and little traffic. Even if the home had indoor plumbing and electricity, Grandma wouldn't have sold it, wanting it to remain in the family.

I parked in the entrance to a farmer's field and walked a quarter mile down the road to the stone house. A rusted metal roof covered the old thatch one. Ivy trailed across the front, entering the dwelling through the glassless windows. Several thick, gnarly vines, inches in diameter, resembled tree branches growing up the side of the house. A weathered red wooden door hung on rusted hinges.

I opened the gated iron fence that surrounded the home and two outbuildings. My chest fluttered every time I stepped onto the land where my Flanagan ancestors had lived since the early eighteen hundreds. I'd once told Grandma I wished the walls could talk and tell me stories. Her response was they *did*. I just needed to make sure I was always listening. After that, every time the wind whistled through the house or a wooden beam creaked, I'd stand still and imagine what stories my ancestors were sharing.

I untied a piece of frayed rope looped through the home's door latch, which kept out animals but not delinquent kids. I stepped inside the musty interior surrounded by faded whitewashed walls covered in green moss. Ivy dangled from the thatched roof, where straw was tucked between wooden-pegged beams. Grandma must have recently checked in on the place. Merely a few beer cans and an empty whiskey bottle littered the dirt floor. I always envisioned my great-grandma spinning wool by the large stone fireplace, a black kettle with potato soup hanging over it.

The fireplace, filled with leaves, twigs, and branches, appeared to be waiting for someone to come home and heat up the damp interior. Grandma had given Biddy and me a set of old pots and pans to play house there. She'd also allowed us to paint a smaller room on one end a peach color. The room still had its wood floor, unlike the main room, which had rotted away. We'd swept the dirt floor with an old broom.

One summer while planting a garden out back, Biddy and I'd uncovered skeletal remains. Freaked out that we'd dug up one of my ancestors, we'd hopped on our bikes and raced home. Upon reaching Grandma's, it'd taken us forever to catch our breath and spit out what had happened. Grandma had laughed, relieved that it hadn't been something worse. It turned out the backyard contained a pet cemetery. I'd still felt bad for having disturbed her dog Lucky or Cashel. Thankfully, this was before Biddy had fallen into the Reillys' grave or she'd never have come back here to play.

After tossing all the litter into a plastic bag, I secured the rope through the door latch and headed back toward the car. A bright-yellow figure approached in the distance. By the time I reached the car, Rosie Connolly came into focus, dressed in tan slacks and a neon-yellow rain jacket and tennies. Not a cloud in the sky, but you never knew when they'd move in and you'd be caught in a torrential downpour.

Rosie greeted me with a wave and a bright smile. "Well, hello, luv. Didn't expect to be meeting anyone out here. Would often run into your grandmother walking—that was about it. Or one of the Caffrey girls out riding horse."

I explained my new caretaker position for the family homestead.

"Your great-grandmother was such a lovely lady. Always had the prettiest flowers along the front of the house."

"I wish I'd known her. Yet Grandma told me so many stories, I feel like I personally knew all my ancestors."

"Even though Sean wasn't a Connolly by blood, he'd still felt an ancestral connection to the family land, which made Paddy pleased as pie."

So Evelyn McCreery was right. Sean had been adopted.

"The foundation of Paddy's grandparents' home is at the back of our property." Rosie smiled, staring off into the fields. "When Sean was young, he'd spend hours back there searching for priceless family heirlooms. Found a ladies' shoe, pieces of a broken ceramic vase, and a few other treasures of little value. He kept them in an old wooden box." Her smile faded as she returned from her trip down memory lane.

I told her the story about Biddy and I finding the pet bones in the backyard.

She laughed. "Bet that put a fright into the two of you."

Before Rosie went on her way, I promised to stop by soon for tart.

I was torn. If Sean was Finn's father, that would entail

having to first find Sean's biological family before trying to connect him to Finn. That would be double the research. That would also mean Stella was Finn's stepmom. Yet if Sean was Finn's father, I couldn't think of a better grandmother for Finn than Rosie Connolly.

And Rosie could certainly use some family.

Twelve

WHEN I'D CONTACTED Edmond about visiting the Lynches, he'd graciously offered to phone Gretta. He'd recalled the daffodil debacle and believed Grumpy Gretta would remember me and still hold a grudge. The flash from the past had given him a good chuckle. Maybe Gretta could also laugh about it now.

When I picked up Edmond, I hadn't even shut off the car and he was out the front door, anxious for our adventure. On our drive there, I reminded him that our pretense for visiting was updating the school reunion's roster and offering Gretta a copy of Finn's photo.

"Can I take a look at the snap again?" Edmond said.

"Sure. The copies are in my purse, but I have it right here on my phone." I brought up the photo.

Edmond studied it. "I see Mickey Molloy in that boy now. At least the lad has this photo to go on."

"And a disconnected phone number on the back." I swiped to the picture of the photo's back.

"Wonder if my friend Mary at the phone company mightn't be able to look up an old number."

"That'd be great. Before I forget, do you know when the Lynches' son died in the States? The fewer questions for Gretta, the better."

Edmond massaged a finger against the side of his nose, pondering the question. "At least twenty, if not thirty, years ago. Never knew the cause. The family was quite secretive about it. He was brought back here for the burial."

"Do you know how Sean Connolly died?"

"Heart attack."

That ruled out Stella having also run him off the road. Didn't mean she hadn't given him the heart attack, intentionally or unintentionally.

The Lynches lived down a narrow road leading nowhere I was ever going. Biddy and I avoided that direction. A stretch of green buds along the roadside would soon be sprouting into perky yellow daffodils.

My heart thumped against my tightened chest. "I wonder if these are the same daffodils Grandma, Biddy, and her mom planted nearly twenty years ago."

"Under good conditions the flowers should outlast us all. Quite hearty, they are."

Unless two eight-year-olds uprooted them all. Gretta had probably nurtured those flowers for years to get such a stretch to grow. Then Biddy and I'd destroyed them in a matter of an hour. I understood the woman's anger, but she was still nasty.

An impressive wrought-iron gate opened to a paved drive leading back to a two-story stone house with a yellow door and window trim. Mature oaks, shrubs, and landscaping covered an acre of mowed grass.

We knocked on the door.

My heart thumped harder.

Gretta answered dressed in gray slacks, a gray cashmere sweater, not a stray silver hair loose from her proper bun. Her thin lips pressed into a pathetic attempt at a smile.

A chill slithered up my back and around my neck, choking off my introduction midsentence. I handed her the pan of chicken with little red potatoes and carrots.

Her gaze narrowed. "Yes, I remember you." She continued standing in the doorway, holding the dish. I feared she might give it back and ask us to leave. She grudgingly stepped aside, allowing us to enter.

She led us into a sunny room the color of daffodils. A painting of the flowers hung over a white marble fireplace. The perky décor was a major contrast to Gretta's drab appearance. Edmond and I sat on a cream-colored sofa. The firm cushions forced you to sit ramrod straight, undoubtedly so guests didn't get too comfy and overstay their welcome. No worries there.

Gretta poured three cups from a floral teapot on the cocktail table. She wasn't completely void of Irish hospitality.

I picked up the delicate china cup, willing my hand not to tremble. If I let her smell fear, I was toast. I took a sip of tea. Rather than the robust, comforting flavor of an Irish breakfast tea, a bitter taste filled my mouth. Had she laced the golden beverage with some untraceable poisonous herb she grew in her garden?

"Tommy is unable to join us?" Edmond asked.

"*Thomas* had other obligations today."

"That's too bad." Edmond gestured to their framed wedding photo on the fireplace mantel. "Is that Galway Bay?"

She gave him a curt nod. "I'm from Salthill, just outside Galway. The boys went to the university there."

I smiled at the photo. "What a lovely area." And a young smiling Gretta looked so lovely I'd never have recognized her.

Her harsh gaze narrowed on Edmond. "You mentioned on the phone you have some questions for the reunion roster."

Enough with the pleasantries.

"Yes. I hope you'll be able to attend," he said.

"I think we have plans."

How did she know they had plans when *I* didn't even know the date?

"I thought it would be nice to keep the reunion going in my grandma's memory," I added.

"Yes, she was quite into the local history."

"Not just local. She helped people around the world with genealogy research."

Gretta's cold stare made me sweat. "Never saw the purpose in looking back. And that was quite an undertaking renovating the schoolhouse into a three-bedroom home. It was a bit disused. Surprised they didn't tear it down and build a new house."

This woman didn't have a sentimental bone in her body. Rather than being relieved that I didn't have to add another "protected" item to the home's sales agreement, I despised this woman even more.

I handed her a photo. "The one on the left is your husband. I thought you might like a copy."

She glared at the photo, then me. "You haven't changed one bit. A little liar just like when you were younger."

My back tensed. A sharp pain radiated from my shoulder and down my spine. I bit my lower lip to keep from yelping out.

"This isn't about the reunion," Gretta snapped. "I was in Castleroche the day that lad was showing this photo to the grocer, who directed him to your house. Don't think I don't know what you two are up to." She thrust the picture at me, and I cautiously accepted it. "It took years, but she finally has her life together. I contacted her, and she has no desire to meet him. It's time you left." She stood and stalked off toward the front door.

I trailed safely behind Edmond down the hallway, the spasm in my back making it difficult to walk.

"I'm sorry we upset you," Edmond said. "But I assure you that wasn't our intention. I'm quite unaware of what you are referring to."

Gretta shook her head. "Shame on you, Edmond Collier. You're no better of a liar than she is." She slammed the door so hard my inner ears vibrated.

Edmond and I exchanged confused looks and walked toward the car in silence. We passed by a bed of green daffodil buds. I fought the urge to yank them from the soil with their roots intact and leave them on the witch's doorstep.

Once in the safety of my car, I heaved a sigh. "What was that about?"

Edmond shook his head. "She was quite passionate about her accusation. I would assume the 'she' Gretta was referring to is her daughter, Maeve, who lives in England."

"How old is she?"

He shrugged. "Midfifties or thereabouts."

"The age of Finn's dad. Do you think Maeve gave a baby up for adoption? So Gretta assumed Finn's Maeve's *son* looking for his *mother*?"

"Suppose it's possible."

"What's the chance that would happen with two children in one family around the same time?"

"Stranger things have occurred."

"I hope not. If that nasty woman is Finn's grandmother, I'm not sure I'd have the heart to tell him." I let out a frustrated groan. "That was a total bust. We found out zilch about her sons and way more than I care to know about her daughter."

"Oh, I disagree." A mischievous glint sparkled in Edmond's eyes. "We found out one important detail. Gretta was from Salthill, which is next to Galway, where her sons attended the university."

I stared blankly at Edmond.

"That phone number on the back of the snap is a Galway number. Meaning Finn's father lived in Galway when he met Finn's mother. Coincidence, perhaps. And perhaps not."

"How do you know that was a Galway number?"

"The preface 91 is the city's code."

Funny that Finn hadn't mentioned that.

Finn's grandpa having grown up near the school didn't mean his sons had. Or maybe they'd wanted to get away from their nasty mother, so they'd attended the university in Galway.

Biddy's dad had also lived in Galway.

When I dropped Edmond off at home, my body was still trembling from the aftershocks of our ghastly visit with Gretta. I declined his invite in for a whiskey or two. In my current state, both mentally and physically, I feared I wouldn't stop at two drinks and be tanked when Biddy and I went to the pub to see the Molloys perform.

A text came through from Biddy.

How'd it go with Gretta?

Horrible.

My phone rang. Biddy.

"Was the witch still upset about her bloody flowers?"

"It couldn't have gone any worse if I'd put her daffodils through a woodchipper. After calling me a little liar, she accused us of trying to help Finn locate his biological *mother*, Gretta's *daughter*."

"What?"

"Seems Gretta was in Castleroche when Finn was showing the photo. However, Gretta seems to think he's looking for his mother, which Edmond and I gathered she believes to be her daughter, Maeve. Did you ever hear about her giving a baby up for adoption?"

"Have never even seen the woman. She's been living in England for as long as I know. But she'd be around my mum's age. When you pick me up tonight, we can ask her."

I didn't mention that Gretta was from Galway and so was the phone number on Finn's photo. In the nineties, Biddy's dad had also owned a pub in Galway. Biddy would become defensive, and that'd get us nowhere.

"I'm going to stop at the cemetery and see if I can locate the grave for the Lynch boy who died in the States. Maybe we can rule him out as a potential father."

"I'll go with you."

I slowed down. "To the cemetery?"

"After visiting Rosie, I decided I need to overcome my fear of cemeteries. Look at you. You went into the goat pen and faced your fear of sheep."

And now I was afraid of sheep *and* goats.

"I feel horrible I didn't attend your grandma's burial. I need to do this. And you need to be with me. Same as my last time in a cemetery."

"I'll pick you up in ten minutes."

I was proud of Biddy's positive and proactive attitude in addressing her fear. After all, she couldn't avoid them forever. It was inevitable that one day some loved ones were going to die.

What were the chances Biddy would fall into a grave twice?

When I picked up Biddy, she had on thigh-high boots. Not the type that made a fashion statement, but the kind that enabled you to traverse streams and creeks without getting soaked. Her dad's green rubber waders he wore fly-fishing. At least she wasn't wearing his waterproof nylon jumpsuit with suspenders.

Biddy lumbered over to the car. She slid onto the front seat and swung her legs around to the inside. The rubber boots made it a bit challenging to bend her knees, but she finally managed.

She held up a hand. "Don't say a word."

"I wasn't going to."

I wouldn't have known where to begin. Except that maybe a licensed therapist should be helping Biddy overcome her fear, rather than me. I was feeling wholly unqualified to deal with her current behavior.

"I read that a physical barrier between you and your fear helps ease your anxiety, making you feel safer."

No clue how to respond, I sat in silence the entire drive to the cemetery while Biddy chatted incessantly about nothing. When I pulled into the dirt drive, the abandoned church's spire rose up to the purplish pink sunset. The downside to winter in Ireland, besides buckets of rain, was the shorter days than in the US. The sun didn't rise until almost 9:00 a.m. and was starting to set at 4:00 p.m. On the flip side, summer was great, when it was light from five in the morning until after ten at night.

"Edmond knows the location of most graves here. He gave me directions to the Lynches'. Will keep us from having to wander around for an hour in the dark searching for it."

We reached the towering wrought-iron gate, and Biddy paused, staring into the cemetery.

"Just coming here is a big step," I said. "Maybe you should hang outside this time and work up to going in next visit."

"What if there isn't a next time? I'm here now, and I'm doing it." With a look of fierce determination, Biddy plodded through the open gate in her oversized wellies.

We took a right at the church, went up five rows, then halfway down to the Lynches' tombstone, exactly where Edmond had said it would be. A massive Celtic cross soared up from a granite stone engraved with Tommy's and Gretta's names and birth dates, death dates pending. However, their son Richard's inscription included both. Born 1968. Died 1987.

"He died before Finn was conceived, so we can cross him off the list," I said.

Two down, seven to go, now that Mickey Molloy had been added to our list.

"How absolutely brill is this?" Biddy beamed with pride. "Here I am standing in the middle of a cemetery." She teared up.

I gave her a hug. "It's totally brill."

She let out a ragged breath. "The only downside is I have Gretta to thank for it. If she wasn't such a bloody witch, refusing to answer your questions, I might not be standing here right now. How mad is that?"

"No way are we giving that woman credit for your progress. Give my grandma credit since you were upset over not attending her burial, or thanks to Rosie's visit."

We headed back toward the entrance. Biddy had a bounce in her step until we spied the *closed* iron gate. She took off running toward the gate, nearly tripping on her oversized boots. She slipped a hand through the iron spindles and tugged on the padlock. Unsuccessful in opening it, she curled her fingers around the spindles and tried shaking them, screaming for someone to let us out.

"They never lock this gate," she said between cries for help.

"You're right—they don't. And why would someone lock it when our car is parked in the drive?"

Biddy snapped her mouth shut, capturing a scream. We slid our panicked gazes toward the cemetery.

Had someone locked us in here on purpose?

Now eerily quiet after Biddy's deafening screams, I could hear a cow moo in the distance and a twig snap nearby, followed by crunching gravel.

Biddy turned and scrambled up the iron gate despite her rubber-soled feet slipping and sliding the entire way. She swung a leg over the top, the back of her jacket catching on a spear-tipped spindle. Freeing herself in seconds flat, she flew down the other side and sprinted toward the car.

Astounded by Biddy's amazing feat, survival mode kicked in. I clambered up the iron gate, pain crippling my shoulder. Scuttling over the top, I made sure my jacket and butt didn't get speared. Halfway down the other side, I leaped to freedom.

The next time Biddy entered a cemetery would undoubtedly be when she took up permanent residence.

Thirteen

UNLIKE THE DRIVE to the cemetery, Biddy didn't utter a word the entire way home.

I pulled up in front of her home on the back side of the pub. "You probably want to pass on going to see the Molloys perform."

"Pick me up in two hours." She stepped from the car and stripped off her waders.

At least this time she wasn't stripping in the middle of the pub.

I went home, wrapped up in my robe, and sat on the couch with a glass of wine, mesmerized by the twinkle lights on the rosebush trellis. After a few sips, I relaxed back on the couch with the wadded ball of paper from behind the fairy door. I peeled away the dried colored paper slips. Too bad the ink had washed out, making them impossible to read. The only wish I could remember having written was wanting to live with Grandma rather than my parents. Yet after I graduated from high school, consumed with wanderlust, I'd decided to travel before settling down in one spot.

As if Grandma would live forever.

I cut up small slips of paper and wrote down two wishes with a permanent marker. Same as any wish, if you shared it with someone, the wish wouldn't come true. Flashlight in hand, wellies on my feet, I hiked across the backyard to the ash tree. I tucked the slips of paper in the hiding space behind the fairy door.

Back inside, I called my real estate agent about preserving the ash tree. Not only did he quit, he refused to recommend another agent. How rude. As if my requests were that unreasonable. The last thing I wanted was a judgmental sales agent. I needed a highly motivated one who could sell the house within five days. Like Shirley Hardyman. You couldn't drive two miles without seeing her smiling face on a *For Sale* sign in someone's yard. Next time I saw one, I'd write down her number.

An hour until I had to pick up Biddy, I popped two ibuprofens for my back pain, threw on jeans and a cute green top, and my brown boots. I applied full makeup for the first time in weeks, maybe months, including penciling in my damaged brow. I wasted a half hour flat ironing my hair, when it would take five minutes for the dampness to turn it frizzy. I stuck a hair clip in my purse as backup.

When I arrived at Biddy's, she and her mom were watching reruns of *Father Ted* while her dad was out front manning the bar. Biddy was laughing at the show and eating chocolate ice cream. You'd never have known that merely a few hours earlier she'd been trapped in a cemetery.

"Mags had an odd conversation with Gretta Lynch today," Biddy told her mom.

Dressed in peach yoga pants and a gray T-shirt, Ita

matched the room's retro eighties peach and mint color scheme nicely. "I thought you girls steered clear of that woman after the daffodils?"

I eased down in a cream-and-peach patterned chair. The overstuffed piece of furniture felt comfy against my sore back. The ibuprofen was kicking in. "We do, but I'm updating my grandma's student roster for the reunion this summer, so Edmond and I went to visit her." I hated lying to Biddy's mom. "She said some strange things that led me to believe her daughter, Maeve, gave a child up for adoption years ago."

Ita nodded. "Straight out of high school, Maeve went to stay with relatives in England. She returned ten months later. It was rumored that she'd had a baby and put it up for adoption."

"Who was the father?" I was being nosy more than anything.

"Supposedly a married man. I'm sure that about gave Gretta a stroke, with her always trying to maintain the facade of a proper family. Maeve was home maybe a year, then returned to England. She rarely comes back, from what I hear."

We were learning juicy, yet irrelevant, family secrets rather than clues to finding Finn's father.

"If you get pregnant before marriage, I'd never kick you out of the house," Ita told Biddy.

"How about you kick me out and keep my kid?"

Ita's gaze sharpened. "You better be giving me grandchildren. Lord knows your sister, Clare, never will." Her features relaxed. "A family must stick together no matter how rough things get."

Would she still feel that way if she discovered her husband, rather than her daughter, was the one with an illegitimate child?

Sitting in my car outside Coffey's pub, Biddy handed me a clump of gray cat fur from a plastic baggie. "Went over and vacuumed under Clare's living room furniture."

"Good thing she's gone, or she'd be wondering why you were cleaning her house." I shoved the fur into my front jeans pockets.

"I'd just tell her I was taking an art class and we were studying textured mediums."

Biddy couldn't make a bowl out of Play-Doh and was too impatient to color within the lines.

"If the guy has a severe allergy, he likely takes meds before going out in public," she said. "So this is a shot in the dark."

"What if he has a serious reaction?"

"I have an EpiPen."

Biddy stabbing someone with an EpiPen in the pub would blow our attempt at being discreet.

"Are we going to talk about what happened earlier?" I said.

"With Aileen's goats?"

"You know what I mean. We can't just ignore it for twenty years like we did the last time."

Biddy let out a massive sigh, dropping back against the seat. "Fine. I wasn't going to bring it up just yet because you're going to think I've gone absolutely mad."

That ship had sailed with the green rubber waders.

"I think...I'm cured."

"Denial isn't good either."

"It's not denial. Seriously. After I got home, instead of drinking the pub outta whiskey, I felt like popping the cork on a champagne bottle. I felt...fearless. Ready to take on another cemetery. Don't get me wrong. I was bloody terrified being locked in there, but it forced me to take control of the situation and save myself. Unlike when I fell in the Reillys' grave, crippled with fear..."

As I recalled, rather than being paralyzed with fear, Biddy had screamed her bloody head off.

"You'd had to rescue me. This time rescuing myself gave me an empowering feeling." Biddy beamed with optimism. "I seriously think I'm better."

I questioned her quick recovery yet congratulated Biddy with a gentle hug, being careful of my shoulder. After all, maybe my skepticism was fueled by envy. Biddy had over-come her fear of cemeteries in record time—after twenty years—whereas I'd *added* goats to my list of fears.

We entered Coffey's pub, where Mickey Molloy and his son Peter sat on stools by the far wall. Mickey on the fiddle, Peter a tin whistle. The lively Irish tune made me want to do a jig. I gave Mickey a wave, and he smiled hello.

Biddy elbowed her way through a cluster of guys blocking the long wooden bar. She flagged down a young guy in a Jameson T-shirt and ordered the Molloys drinks. The bartender returned with a pint of Guinness, then grabbed a bottle from the back bar and poured a golden-colored liquor into a glass.

"What's that?" I asked.

"Keegans."

Biddy and I exchanged smiles.

Finn's father's favorite whiskey.

"That's Peter's. The jar's Mickey's."

Peter drank Keegans? Hmm...

Biddy and I ordered cider ale and paid for the drinks. With Ireland's stiff drunk-driving laws, that'd be it for us. The Molloys finished the tune, and I presented their drinks.

"Thanks a mil, luv." Mickey introduced me to his son, a proud glint in his bright-blue eyes. His eyes that reminded me of Finn's and his son Peter's, who was a spitting image of his father, except a few inches shorter and his salt-and-pepper hair hadn't gone completely white.

Peter raised his whiskey. "Sláinte."

We all joined in the toast.

Neither of the men were fighting back sneezes or watering eyes. Hmm...

"Do you know any Beatles tunes?" I asked.

"Ah, that we do," Mickey said. "How about 'Maggie Mae'?" He gave me a wink.

Biddy's dad's nickname for me.

"I thought Rod Stewart sang that?"

"That he did, but a different version," Peter said. "The Beatles was a take on an old folk song about a prostitute robbing a sailor returning from sea."

My gaze darted to Biddy. "My nickname is about some hooker mugging a sailor?"

Biddy shrugged. "I'm sure it was Rod Stewart's version, not the Beatles, my dad was referring to."

Otherwise that meant her father was an even bigger Beatles fan than she'd thought, familiar with some obscure Beatles tune. Same as Finn's dad.

"Doubt most people know the Beatles' version," Peter said. "Only thirty-nine seconds long, it was the second shortest song on a Beatles album. It was a tongue-in-cheek version they sang in a thick Scouse accent they once did while warming up in the studio."

Peter was a huge Beatles fan, drank Keegans, had Finn's eyes, and was much closer to Finn's mother's age than Mickey.

He had to be Finn's father.

"You sound like a Beatles expert," Biddy said. "Have you ever been to Liverpool? We're thinking of visiting."

Peter nodded. "Several times to visit The Cavern Club, where the Beatles first played."

"As I said, I played a few pubs there," Mickey said. "We best get playing *here*. What would ya like to be hearing if not 'Maggie Mae'?"

"How about 'In My Life'?"

"One of my favorites." Mickey set his pint on the bar rail along the wall, then selected an acoustic guitar.

A couple vacated a nearby cocktail table. Biddy and I swooped in and snagged it.

"No sneezing or wheezing from either of them, but they are definitely high on the list of candidates," I said.

"Some people's allergies fade over time, or maybe they took meds."

Or like Finn said, maybe the guy just hadn't liked cats. I wasn't going to say that and get a rise out of Biddy over her dad disliking felines.

"Is Mattie Molloy here?"

Biddy scanned the room, shaking her head. "I'll check out the other side of the bar back by the loo." She did a quick walk through and returned with a smile. "No Mattie, but Tommy Lynch is over there."

"Gretta's hubby?"

Biddy nodded.

My upper back spasmed, and I massaged my shoulder. "What if she told him about my visit?"

"Let's find out." Biddy headed across the bar with her ale.

I reluctantly followed, hoping the man was nothing like his nasty wife.

Biddy smiled at a gray-haired man with a bit of a belly and happy *brown* eyes. "Mind if we be snagging the seats behind ya?"

Tommy stood and swept a hand toward the red upholstered bench. "Not a' tall. Would never turn away two lovely lasses."

My back tension relaxed at the man's warm welcome.

When Biddy introduced us, no recognition or anger registered on his face. Best not to mention my visit if his wife hadn't. Did I dare share Finn's photo with him? Gretta would flip out if he brought it home. Too bad I couldn't be there to witness her meltdown.

"The Molloys are quite talented, aren't they?" Biddy said.

Tommy nodded. "Ian dabbled in the fiddle but didn't stick with it. Don't recall if Rory ever played an instrument or not."

Finn hadn't mentioned whether his father had been a *good* fiddle player.

"Rory still in Navan?" Biddy asked.

Tommy nodded. "He's selling homes there. Ian's farming."

My ears perked up. "He's a real estate agent?"

Not only was I in the market for a new agent, but that would give me an excuse to meet Rory Lynch. I told Tommy about needing a sales agent.

"Ah, right," he said. "You be selling the schoolhouse. Thought ya had some interested buyers."

"They fell through." I told him about the radiators, boiler, and everything else that needed fixing.

"I could be giving the heating system a look."

"I can't afford to fix the place up."

"Would only charge for replacements or parts, not for labor. I'll call in and take a look. We can go from there. Don't mind helping to keep the schoolhouse in good form. Four generations of Lynches studied there. Maggie should have mentioned the radiators. I'd have helped her out."

"My grandma preferred a more rustic lifestyle."

"Being a genealogist, living like her ancestors put her in their mindset, I'd suppose."

I'd never thought of it that way before.

This was a perfect segue to discussing the photo. I slipped it from my purse and handed it to Tommy.

He smiled. "Haven't seen that snap in a while."

Why? Was it missing from his family photo album because a son had given it to Finn's mom?

"I'd be loving a copy. Not sure if I have one." His smile widened. "Charlie was a cute little fella."

I was about to ask if Charlie had been his or Mickey's dog, but Biddy smacked my leg under the table. She discreetly nodded toward Finn standing by the entrance, holding a duffel bag, resembling a drifter passing through. A beaten-up stranger looking to make a few bucks on a boxing match behind the pub so he could move on to the next rural village. Curious gazes peered over at him, likely wondering how this guy's opponent had fared.

"Jaysus," Biddy muttered. "When checking on him earlier, I mentioned we'd be here tonight listening to music. Didn't think he'd be showing up. Doctor wasn't releasing him until tomorrow."

Spying us, Finn headed in our direction.

If he were too inquisitive, he'd blow it.

I excused myself. Passing by a Jameson mirror, I noticed a few stray strands of hair and tucked them behind my ear as I intercepted Finn. "Showing up here in your condition isn't being discreet. We should go." I grasped hold of his elbow to direct him toward the door, but he wouldn't budge.

"My snap's missing." Desperation filled his voice, weighted with exhaustion. "It was in my jacket pocket before the accident. I'm sure of it. The person who stole it is likely the same one who put me in the hospital. The person who doesn't want me finding my father."

"I know it's not the same, but I have copies." I glanced around nervously. "Let's not discuss it here."

"And here's another Beatles song for Mags and Biddy." Mickey's voice carried over the sound system, competing with the loud chattering.

Finn quirked a curious brow and headed across the bar toward the musicians. Biddy and I were hot on his heels.

Mickey's gaze locked with Finn's; a curious glint shone in the man's blue eyes. Over the fact that Finn looked like he'd just had a brawl in the parking lot or that he had the same bright-blue eyes as himself?

"Is that fella a possibility?" Finn's gaze was still focused on Mickey, who was now eyeing his fiddle. "Do you think he's the one who stole my photo and ran me off the road?"

"No, I don't. But does he look familiar?"

"Yeah. He looks a bit like me."

I grasped hold of Finn's elbow once again. "I'll tell you everything I know. I promise."

Biddy shot me a warning look not to mention her father.

I wasn't sure how much longer I could keep my promise.

Actually, had I ever even made that promise?

Fourteen

BIDDY HOPPED in the backseat of my car, Finn in the front. She sprang forward on the seat, poking her head between us. "Let's wait to see if anyone follows us out, curious about Finn."

We stared straight ahead at the pub. The door opened and Peter Molloy exited, glancing around.

Biddy let out an excited squeal. "He's looking for us."

Peter lit a cigarette.

"Or he's taking a smoking break," I said.

"Who exactly is the fella?" Finn asked.

I gave him the skinny on the Molloys.

Finn nodded. "Look a bit like them, I'd say. Remind me to show you a snap of my mum when we get to your house."

"What if you send your mum a snap of the Molloys?" Biddy said. "Maybe she'd recognize one of them."

"If she finds out I'm looking for my father, she'll be raging. She feels he made his choice years ago and to let it rest. Yet he hadn't known about *me* years ago."

"Did your mom ever mention his age?"

Finn shook his head. "This is about the older fiddle player?"

I shrugged. "Can't rule him out. You have their same bright-blue eyes." I sounded obsessed with Finn's eyes. "But a lot of Irish have bright-blue eyes."

Slightly frazzled, I pulled out of the parking lot.

"Who was the man you were talking to when I came in?"

"Tommy Lynch. Haven't spoken to either of his sons yet. Out of nine possibilities, we've ruled out two. One who died in 1987 and one who has a life partner. That's the good news."

"What's the bad news?"

"One possibility died five years ago."

And if Finn's father turned out to be Biddy's dad, it might destroy her family.

"It's also not good news that someone in my family isn't keen to meet me."

"Whoever ran you off the road might not even be related. The person might have acted on impulse out of anger, assuming you were the result of an affair."

Finn's gaze narrowed. "You think a *woman* ran me off the road?"

I hadn't said that, had I?

"I don't know anything for sure. We can't jump to conclusions." Even though that was all Biddy and I'd been doing the past few days. "We need to tread lightly."

Finn shook his head in frustration. "Maybe it's time I flat out ask the men if they mightn't be my father."

"You have to lie low or another attempt might be made on your life."

"I've been lying low in the hospital for days. I want to help. He's *my* father."

"You're right. But you need to be careful. And it's not fair to your father if everyone in town knows about you. That's his, and your, business. Nobody else's. You'll have the chance to meet at least two of the men at the tractor run tomorrow." My gaze darted to Biddy in the backseat. "I totally zoned that we have to make twenty-five sandwiches for tomorrow."

"Can get plenty of eggs from my mum's hens for egg mayonnaise. I can pop into Tesco in the morning for bread and sandwich meat."

When I was eight, I spent Easter break with Grandma. Biddy had never heard of dying Easter eggs. Trying to dye her mom's brown eggs was too difficult, but we hid them anyway. I had forgotten the eggs needed to be hard-boiled. We'd found all but two of the raw eggs. Months later, the stench of rotting eggs gave away their hiding spots.

"That'd be great," I said. "We can make them at my house."

"I'll be paying for them." Finn slipped a bill from his wallet and handed it to Biddy.

"See how you're feeling in the morning before ya decide if you're attending," Biddy said. "You need to be taking it easy. You should still be in the hospital."

I pulled into the drive at home.

"I'll get the gate." Biddy secured the padlock, standing outside the iron gate. "I must crack on—lots to do. See ya tomorrow."

Lots to do at eleven o'clock at night?

"You can't walk home." *And you can't leave me alone*

with Finn! "It's dark out. You'll get hit by some crazy driver leaving your pub."

"I have a torch." She slipped a small flashlight from her purse, handy for all the trips between our places. "Will be here by ten to make sandwiches." She followed the yellow beam of light up the road.

Inside, dying embers remained from the roaring fire I'd made three hours ago. "Sorry it's so cold. Radiators aren't working right." I banged a fist against the temperamental one, and instead of hissing, it wheezed. I gave it another hit. "Had an offer from someone to fix them, but I'm selling the house as is. Can't afford to be repairing everything beforehand."

Finn snapped his head back in surprise. "Selling the place, are ya?"

I nodded. "It's too much for me to keep up."

"Don't think you can make a go of it? Seems like you belong in Ireland."

"I start a new job in the States next week."

His eyes dimmed. "That's too bad."

That I was leaving or that I had to sell Grandma's place?

"Was hard losing your granny, I'm sure. Can't imagine when my granny passes. Was pretty much raised by my grand-parents."

I wished I'd been raised by my grandma. Except I'd have missed my dad.

"I'll change the sheets on the upstairs bed. Are you able to walk up the steps?" I didn't want to put him in Grandma's bed. I hadn't been able to bring myself to strip the sheets and quilt after the wake.

He nodded. "I appreciate you helping me when you

barely know me. Most women would have been scared off by someone trying to kill me."

"I know what it's like searching for your biological father." I told him about my DNA discovery and how my mother was no longer alive to answer my questions. "At least you have a photo to go on. I have a third cousin DNA match, which means we share two-time great-grandparents. My father could be one of hundreds of their descendants. I've only known a year, and I'm already frustrated and disheartened over trying to find him. I can't imagine what it's been like not knowing your father's identity your entire life."

"The hardest part was my mother refusing to discuss him except for those few details. Not that she knew much about him, but she never cared to find him after he ignored her messages. Sometimes I wonder if we're better off not knowing."

"Yeah. If I hadn't taken that test on a whim, I'd never have known. Neither would my dad. I confronted him in anger, assuming he'd known he wasn't my father. He hadn't a clue and couldn't even guess at my biological father's identity. I regretted telling him. No reason for us both to be angry with my mother, since she was gone. My dad's encouraging, even though it's a bit awkward. I've never told my sisters."

Would just be one more thing for them to not care about.

"Hopefully both our fathers are still out there so they can provide us some closure," he said.

"Maybe we should start a DNA support group."

He laughed. "Seriously, that's a grand idea. If we can't determine my father's identity by nosing around, perhaps my new DNA test will provide more information than the last one. But unless it's a first cousin, I wouldn't know where to begin."

"I can help. As long as you at least share great-grandparents, there's a good chance of figuring out the connection. And I already started the four men's family trees, so we can cross-check any surname matches from your DNA results."

The exhaustion vanished from Finn's face, and his eyes flickered with interest. "Can I see the trees?"

"I've only started two. They're a work in progress. But if we aren't successful in locating your father before I leave for Maine, I promise I'll have the trees finished by the time you get your results." As upset as Finn was earlier about discovering his missing photo, I wasn't providing him a list of possible suspects to confront.

Finn smiled. "Thanks." He slipped his wallet from his back pocket. "Need to show you that snap of my mum." He thumbed through the plastic photo sleeves. His gaze narrowed on an empty one. "It's gone. Jaysus. Why would someone also have stolen that snap?"

Oh boy. The woman in the photo had looked so young. More like a girlfriend than a mother.

"Does she have long dark hair and you guys are standing in front of a lake?"

Finn quirked a curious brow.

I removed the photo from my purse and handed it to him. "I swear I didn't take the other one." To further convince him, I explained that I'd been checking his wallet, in front of a nurse, for his father's photo. When I hadn't found it, I'd taken this one, not wanting to look suspicious.

He nodded, accepting my explanation, slipping the photo back into its spot.

"She's quite pretty. You don't have her green eyes, and you obviously get your height from your father."

"Speaking of green"—Finn's gaze slid down to my green chiffon blouse, causing my heart to go berserk—"that color is brilliant on you." He raised his gaze, staring into my eyes.

His thick dark lashes made his eyes look even bluer... Those eyes that reflected so much emotion. I'd never met a guy who discussed his feelings so openly.

My breathing quickened. I forced my gaze from Finn's and up the staircase. "I'll go change the sheets." I escaped upstairs to the office. I searched the hot press cupboard for a set of clean sheets, my mind racing.

Finn was totally hot, but neither of us were in the right place for a relationship. I was heading back to the States, while Finn would remain in Ireland. However, he must go to the States on occasion to visit his mother...

Knock it off!

We were both merely feeling vulnerable. Finn recovering from a near-death experience, me from Grandma's death and preparing to sell her house. Or maybe it was my imagination and Finn was feeling *nothing*. The attraction was merely one sided. If my failed relationship with Josh had taught me anything, it was that I was not falling for a guy based solely on a physical attraction. However, Finn and I also had bonded over genealogy research and the desire to locate our biological fathers. A bond that would likely weaken once we discovered his father's identity.

I wanted a guy who made me laugh. Someone who shared my dry, often peculiar sense of humor. Like Biddy. We were so in tune, always knowing what the other was thinking. We could express our feelings without judging each other. And whenever we...

Omigod. Was that what I was looking for in a guy?

Biddy?

Or was this telling me that I might as well give up on ever finding a guy with all the qualities I'd find in a girlfriend? That I either had to lower my standards or I'd be a spinster and Biddy's roomie in my old age?

I refused to settle. I would find Biddy in a man. Except it'd be wonderful to have one who also liked to cook and clean.

Fifteen

FINN, Biddy, and I arrived in Drumcara an hour before the tractor run. New, old, and vintage tractors filled O'Sullivan's large lot and trailed down the four streets at the crossroads. Biddy snagged a spot in a church lot a quarter mile up the road.

"Is this your first tractor run?" Biddy asked Finn.

He shook his head. "My grandfather farmed and often participated in runs. I rode along when I was younger. Was great craic."

I couldn't picture Finn on a tractor. He was definitely more the BMW type. I also could never have pictured him in makeup. Biddy's foundation and face powder were a shade lighter than Finn's skin tone. The makeup attracted attention to his bruises rather than concealing them. This was rural Ireland, not opening night on Broadway.

"Where did you live?" I asked.

"Ballycarney. A small townland just outside Wexford."

I also would have thought of him as more of a city guy.

I nodded. "I've been there."

He looked surprised. "Seriously? Nobody has ever been there outside of people in Wexford."

"There's a cute little church right off the main road. My grandma and I were down there researching Cullens. Met a Donald Cullen, who owned an auto shop."

He smiled. "I know Donald. Nice fella. I was on a hurling team with him."

We headed toward the pub, platters of sandwiches in hand, cat fur in Biddy's and my jeans pockets. By the time we reached O'Sullivan's, two dogs and a cat were trotting along behind, sniffing us out.

Finn glanced over his shoulder at the animals. "Friendly little yokes here."

I fessed up about the fur.

Finn laughed. "I guess you're taking my search seriously."

Several tractors in the parking lot hummed to life, vibrating through my chest. Biddy waved hello to fellas chatting next to a tractor with colorful strings of lights twinkling around its massive tire rims. We headed into the pub. A young guy behind the bar was serving a handful of patrons. After the run, it would be packed with thirsty farmers.

We followed a woman carrying bags of chips into a side room. A sheet of wood protected a pool table top, converting it into a buffet with soup and coffee urns, bowls of munchies, and one lonely platter of tuna fish sandwiches. We added our four sandwich trays to the feast.

George walked in opening a package of napkins and smiled at Finn. "Ah, glad to see you're on the mend. Was worried about ya." He shook Finn's hand.

"I'm grand. Feeling much better than I look."

"Help yourself to coffee or tea. If you'd be liking something a bit stronger, it's on the house."

"Might take ya up on that," Finn said.

"No drinking with the meds ya must be taking," Biddy said.

Finn smiled. "I best listen to my nurse."

I eyed George's Springsteen T-shirt. "Now that's a no-brainer. I could name at least twenty songs."

He gave me a thumbs-up. "Slane Castle, 1985."

"Saw the Stones there in 2007," Finn said.

"Ah, did ya now? Might have seen me there also. Saw 'em there in '82 and 2007. We'll catch up more later." He gave Finn a pat on the back and headed out to the bar area.

"Nice fella," Finn said. "I was a bit down when I was here showing the snap around. He was a good listener."

George had provided me with some great insight on Stella.

"Would ya mind passing around these biscuits?" A woman gestured to trays of chocolate chip and ginger cookies.

Finn, Biddy, and I each grabbed a tray and headed toward the front door. I stepped outside and nearly slammed into Stella carrying a platter of cupcakes. We literally kept running into each other.

Her eyes widened in surprise at the sight of Finn. Was she surprised to see him *here* or *alive*? A nervous smile twitched the corners of her mouth. So much for her previous cool-as-a-cucumber demeanor.

The woman was guilty.

"Ah, good to see you up and about." She grimaced at Finn's bruised face or maybe Biddy's horrible makeup job. "Looks a might painful."

"Looks worse than they feel," he said.

"Ah, that's grand." She sounded relieved. Too relieved? Was guilt taking its toll on the woman? "I best drop these off." She escaped inside the pub.

"Does she look familiar?" I asked Finn.

He nodded. "Works across the street, I believe."

I led him off to the side of the building for privacy while Biddy circulated. "She was Sean Connolly's wife. A possible father."

Finn smiled, glancing around. "Is he here?"

I gave him a sympathetic look. "He's the man who passed away a few years ago."

His smiled faded. "Was she the one you thought reacted in a jealous rage without knowing if she had a reason?"

I nodded. He needed to know Stella might have run him off the road so he could watch his back. Yet if I told him I'd caught her fleeing his hospital room, he'd surely confront her about the photo. We needed the element of surprise on our side to catch her.

"If he was your father, there's a wee challenge. He was adopted."

"Then let's hope he wasn't. Except it would be interesting that neither of us would have known our biological fathers."

"If it comes down to it, maybe Sean's mother, Rosie, could have the adoption records opened. They might provide Sean's biological parents' information."

We joined Biddy, who was talking to a guy with graying hair.

"Oh, hiya," Biddy said. "Was just telling Ian Lynch here that we saw his father at the pub last night."

Same as his father, Ian's brown eyes and small build—except for a bit of a beer belly—didn't resemble Finn one bit.

"Your father is so sweet," I said. "He offered to repair the radiators and boiler at my grandma's house at cost."

"Ah, Maggie Flanagan's granddaughter, are ya? Heard ya be selling the place."

I nodded. "Haven't found buyers yet."

He rubbed his stubbly chin. "Might be knowing an interested couple. My friend's son was recently married. Would be the perfect starter home for 'em. And they're local. Not some blow-in from Dublin."

"Is that Siobhan and Dylan Farrell?" Biddy asked.

He nodded.

Biddy smiled at me. "They'd be perfect for your granny's home."

So why wasn't I jumping for joy?

"Do you think your brother Rory might be interested in representing the house?" I asked.

"Let's find out."

Ian called his brother, who confirmed he'd be happy to show the house to the couple tomorrow if that worked for everyone. Excellent. That provided me the perfect opportunity to get insight into Rory. Yet that meant in twenty-four hours Grandma's house might be sold and I'd be without a home. An icky feeling tossed my tummy. I could always crash at Biddy's when I came to Ireland. However, driving past Grandma's house would likely induce a panic attack, especially if it no longer looked like her home. What if the new owners painted the exterior gray or some other depressing color!

"I was just asking Ian if he'd ever been to Liverpool,

seeing as we're considering going," Biddy said.

He shook his head. "Sorry. Never even been to England. Visited a friend in Glasgow a few times. Rory used to date a Welsh girl. Ask him about Liverpool when you see him."

Oh, I planned to.

An announcement requested drivers report to their tractors. Ian wished me luck on the sale of Grandma's house and headed off.

"Scratch Ian Lynch from the possible father list," Biddy said. "Three down and six to go."

"Didn't figure it was him," Finn said. "I've always felt I would have an immediate connection with my father. An innate bond. Like we'd cross paths on the street or in a pub and I'd instinctively know he was my father. The past two weeks, every time I entered a pub, I prepared myself that he might be sitting there having a pint. I'd show him the snap, and it'd slowly register with him who I am. Without a word we'd hug for the first time."

Tears welled up in my eyes.

Biddy fanned her face, fighting back tears. "That is one of the most touching things I've ever heard a man say."

Finn was so not your typical man. However, he almost made me cry more than he made me laugh.

He discreetly nodded toward a group of guys admiring a shiny new green-and-yellow John Deere. "That fella in the tan jacket was here that day I was showing the snap."

"That's Mattie Molloy," Biddy said. "The son of the fiddler at the pub last night. A possible father candidate."

"Why would he hang out at a pub ten miles from his home, with the strict drunk-driving laws?" I mused.

Biddy shrugged. "Haven't a clue." Her gaze darted to me.

"Is *that* a clue?"

"Do you recall talking to him?" I asked Finn.

He nodded. "He was the last person I spoke to before my accident."

We didn't have the chance to question Mattie Molloy before the tractors left on their parade through the rural countryside. Upon returning an hour later, everyone hit the food buffet and bar. We circulated outside with sandwiches, waiting for Mattie to wander out of the packed building for a smoke.

Eyelids heavy from exhaustion, Finn dropped down on a green picnic bench. "Like I said, when I showed Mattie Molloy the snap, he merely gave me directions to your place. No reminiscent smile recalling the night spent with a beautiful, mysterious Irish woman, wondering what ever happened to her. And he didn't check the back of the snap for his phone number. Being taken off guard, I don't think he could have hidden his reaction that well."

"Maybe he's a great poker player," I said. "In the early nineties he studied in Manchester, near Liverpool."

Biddy placed a hand on Finn's shoulder. "You look wrecked. As your nurse, I'm advising you to go home and get some rest."

He shrugged it off, standing. "I'm grand."

"Not for long," I said.

Gretta Lynch marched across the street toward the pub, dressed in a gray wool coat and black slacks. Clouds moved in, and the temperature seemed to drop fifty degrees. Starting to sweat, I held my breath. Was she going to confront me about the photo her husband had brought home last night? Nose in the air, she blew past us and into the pub.

I exhaled some serious air. "Was sure she was going to scratch my eyes out over the photo I gave her husband."

"Must be here to drag Tommy's butt home," Biddy said. "Seen her do it at our pub a dozen times. He's smashed."

"Are those Ian Lynch's parents?" Finn's hesitant tone was laced with dread.

I nodded with a sympathetic smile. "The Lynches are the least likely candidates right now."

A look of relief washed over Finn.

Mattie Molloy moseyed outside with whiskey-glazed eyes, not nearly as blue as his father's and brother's. Lighting a cigarette, he noticed Finn. "Aye, looking a bit worse than the last time I saw ya."

Finn nodded. "Had a bit of an accident."

Mattie's eyes widened. "That was you, outside of town here a few days back? I was here when someone came in and told about the accident. Glad to see you're on the mend." His concern sounded genuine. "I see you met the owner of the schoolhouse."

Finn nodded. "That I did."

"We learned one boy in the photo is your father," I said.

Mattie smiled. "Is it now? Don't recall ever having seen the snap. My father might be liking a copy."

"I gave him one."

"Ah, that's grand."

"Your mum mentioned you studied in Manchester," Biddy said. "Ever make it to Liverpool while you were there? We're thinking of visiting."

Mattie nodded faintly, scratching his stubbly chin. "Probably. I don't quite recall at the moment."

A bit of whiskey fog?

He sneezed, snubbing out the cigarette butt in the ashtray on the table. "Come on in. I'll buy ya all a pint." He buried his nose in the crook of his arm, catching a series of sneezes. "Sorry. Don't know what suddenly came over me."

Biddy, Finn, and I exchanged intrigued looks.

"Allergies?" Biddy said.

"Suppose it could be." He headed inside without identifying his allergy.

"You guys go on," I said. "I'll save the bench."

Biddy hung back. "Allergies often run in the family. Mickey might also have them, if that's indeed why Mattie's sneezing." She gave me a sly grin and scooted inside.

A handful of men were in the lot smoking and chatting. I sat on the picnic table, munching on a ginger cookie. I peered around, spotting Stella's red car at the far end of the convenience store lot. The store was dark inside. I strolled over to take a peek. Maybe the body shop had overlooked damage under the front bumper. No need to get down on my knees for a closer look. The scrapes of blue paint on the dented bumper were plain as day even at dusk.

George had apparently been wrong. Stella hadn't gotten her car repaired. Before I could pull out my phone to snap a shot of the evidence, a hard blow to the back of my head sent a thumping pain radiating down my neck to my sore shoulder. Everything went black, and I collapsed onto the ground.

Head throbbing, the taste of blood in my mouth, I squinted into the darkness. I swept my tongue gently across my swollen lip. The hit to the back of my head had caused me to bite down on my lower lip. I flinched at a sharp pain in my side from a branch poking me in the ribs. I moved it, and thorns prickled my fingers. I was lying in a wall of shrubs.

Better than being tied up in Stella's trunk, bouncing around while she sped down some deserted road to dump my body.

Sitting up caused my head to start spinning. Bracing one hand against the cold ground, I gently placed the other one on the back of my head, finding a large goose egg. When I finally dared to stand, I rocked back on my heels, off balance. Lampposts cast light on my surroundings. I was in the shrub fence between the convenience store and the row of townhouses. Across the street, O'Sullivan's parking lot had thinned out.

How long had I been unconscious?

I walked toward the pub, massaging my temples, trying to make the thumping headache go away. Nearing the building, I winced at the loud voices and music pouring out an open window. I headed inside without having to squeeze between people. Biddy was alone at a corner cocktail table, talking on the phone. Upon spotting me, she hung up and flew over.

"Where have you been?" she demanded.

"Napping out in the bushes."

"You could have told us. We've been looking all over for ya." She waved Finn over from his conversation with George at the bar.

"I wasn't napping on purpose."

Biddy took me by the arm and ushered me outside, where I sat on the picnic bench. I recounted the traumatic event up to the point where I regained consciousness lying in a shrub. "Stella obviously saw me snooping around her car. Now it's gone. I didn't get a shot of the blue paint on the front bumper."

"Quite bold of her with so many people around." Biddy felt the back of my head. "That bump is massive. What'd she whack you with, a tire iron? Thankfully, no open wound. The head has loads of blood vessels. The only way to often stop the bleeding is to cauterize it."

I flinched. Having my scalp burned sounded more painful than having a sliver of my eyebrow singed off.

She took a few steps back and raised her hand. "How many fingers am I holding up?"

"Two."

"Where are you?"

"O'Sullivan's pub in Drumcara."

"Where do you live?"

"Ballycaffey."

She gasped. "You said Ballycaffey. You could have said Florida or Chicago, but you said Ballycaffey."

"What does that mean?"

"That you shouldn't be selling your granny's house."

I rolled my eyes. "Can we please stay focused on Stella attacking me."

Biddy nodded. "Yeah, she's getting more daring."

"Exactly why I'm heading back to Wexford in the morning." Finn's firm tone said case closed.

I sprang to my feet, and the parking lot started spinning.

I planted a hand against the picnic table, steadying myself. "You can't go back."

"This has gotten way too dangerous."

"We now have proof it's Stella," I said. "Even if she gets the bumper fixed, the police can talk to the body shop. You can file charges."

"Which is exactly why I'm *not* pursuing it. It's one thing for Stella to have seen my photo and acted in a jealous rage, assuming I was the son of her late husband and a mistress. But for her to make an attempt on *your* life, she's over the edge. Who knows what she might do next?" He tossed his hands in the air. "She must be confident that Sean was my father to take such a risk."

I shook my head. "She doesn't have to be confident about anything. Maybe the woman's nuts. You can't be certain your father is Sean. If he is, I'm sure his mother, Rosie, would love to meet you. To have a grandson. You'd inherit the Connolly property." And likely Stella's grave plot.

"I don't care about the inheritance. I wouldn't want Rosie to go through the drama of her son's wife attempting to kill his son."

"I think Stella going to prison would make Rosie quite pleased. Besides, we can't let Stella get away with attempted murder. I'm sure as hell not. I could have died from a head injury."

"Still could," Biddy said.

My gaze darted to Biddy. "Why would you say that?"

Concern crinkled her brow. "It's true. You could have bleeding on the brain or other damage." She sounded way more concerned than the goat breaking my back.

My heart raced.

"You need to be going in for tests," she said. "Even a mild bump or contusion can ultimately lead to death."

"See." Finn raked a frustrated hand through his dark hair. "I'm not going to die."

Was I? My heart was going berserk.

"She won't come after you if she knows I'm gone."

"You're so close to finding your father, how can you just quit? I've only been curious about my real father for a year, and I wouldn't give up!"

Finn's gaze darkened. "It's my choice to make. And I choose to stop. My mother was right. There's a good reason my father didn't return her calls, and it's best to let it rest." His jaw tightened. "Promise me you won't pursue this any further."

As if he was being heroic by giving up. Helping me nail that witch would be heroic. Thank God I hadn't penciled in my eyebrow for this guy.

"No way!" My entire body was shaking with anger. "What about me? My life was put in danger too. Like Biddy said, I could still die. I want vengeance. Sorry. I'm not as forgiving as you."

Finn's cheeks reddened.

I held his gaze, my lips pressed firmly together.

His gaze darkened, and a growl vibrated in his throat. Blinking first, he turned and stormed off down the street toward Biddy's car.

Biddy placed a calming hand on my arm. "We need to get you to the hospital."

I was starting to wish I'd stayed in the shrubs.

Sixteen

THE FOLLOWING MORNING, I rolled off the couch at 7:00 a.m. after a two-hour nap. Biddy and I had gotten home from the hospital two hours earlier to find Finn gone. His note said he hated goodbyes. He'd called a taxi to take him to a car rental company to drive home. He apologized for the pain he'd caused me mentally and physically, and especially for our argument. I felt bad about having lost my cool, but I still believed I had the right to pursue justice for myself anyway.

Every inch of my upper body ached, including the goat hoof imprint on my right shoulder. According to the CT scan, I had no internal head injuries. The doctor had advised me to limit my activity. As if I could do that when I only had a few more days to pack up Grandma's house before leaving for Maine. Staying awake and lucid at the hospital hadn't been easy when I was suffering from exhaustion and a thumping headache. Biddy's incessant chatting to keep me awake hadn't helped either. Neither had the fact that my hospital visit had maxed out my credit card.

I gently touched my swollen lip. Luckily, I hadn't bitten off my tongue, so I could give Stella a piece of my mind and an invoice for my ER visit. Yet rather than giving her a heads-up, I should go straight to the police and file charges. However, lacking evidence and credibility—after my Little Red Riding Hood theory—I needed a picture of the bumper, if she hadn't already taken her car in for repairs. Since she hadn't been hiding it, she must not have realized I suspected her of running Finn off the road. Or consumed with guilt, she'd wanted to get caught? Then why whack me over the head? Maybe she'd feel enough remorse to at least return Finn's only memento of his father's family.

The thought of that woman made my head and shoulder throb even worse. I popped two ibuprofens, tossed my hair up in a clip, and threw on jeans and a green sweatshirt with a smiling grizzly bear that read *Grin and Bear It*. Whenever I was in a funk and thought life couldn't suck any worse, I wore this sweatshirt to remind myself that it could. I'd bought it the summer I worked my worst job ever: a housekeeper at a Colorado mountain resort. No person should have to clean somebody else's guest room unless they're wearing a hazmat suit.

My worst experience was the day I'd entered a room to find a murder. I'd watched enough CSI and criminal shows to recognize a crime scene. Refusing to be arrested as an accessory to murder or for obstructing evidence, I marched into the resort manager's office and quit. I hopped the first plane to my dad's in Florida.

I trudged upstairs to the office. The framed photo of Grandma and I sharing an umbrella at the reunion, smiling despite gale-force winds, brought tears to my eyes. I removed it from the wall and placed it on the desk with everything I planned to store at Biddy's until I could afford to ship it home.

Home...wherever that was going to be.

Boxing up Grandma's computer and printer to take to Edmond was my breaking point. Tears flowing down my cheeks, I dropped onto my small desk chair. I plucked Kleenex from a tissue box. Best to get it out of my system before seeing Edmond. Grandma had wanted him to have her computer with research information, historical documents...and school reunion info.

I still had to host a reunion this summer for both Edmond's and my sake. It would make telling Edmond goodbye a bit easier. I blew through a half dozen tissues, wiped my eyes, and shook it off. *Stay strong for Edmond.*

I pushed several boxes off to the side of the room. It needed to look halfway presentable when Rory Lynch brought the couple by for the showing this afternoon. I'd run out of boxes, so genealogy records and books still filled the shelves. Biddy's dad had been saving boxes from deliveries. I'd have to make a pub run.

First, I checked my email to find one from the B & B in Maine with a forty-two-page document detailing my role and responsibilities. I closed the file. An email from Ancestry.com advised me that I had a new DNA match. A second cousin, meaning we likely shared great-grandparents.

My closest match to date.

Heart racing, I logged into my account. I quickly determined the person was a paternal match. Simon Reese was a fifty-four-year-old male living in Cornwall, England. His location wasn't a clue, since descendants of my great-grandparents could be spread out all over the world. However, his name sounded English, and Cornwall was on my bucket list. His private tree contained over five hundred people. The fact that he wasn't attempting to hide his identity with some obscure profile name and no personal details was promising.

He'd likely be open to sharing his private tree.

I clicked on his message button.

I tapped a finger against the keyboard. Should I be vague?

Hey Simon, You are a top match of mine on Ancestry.com. I'm curious how we might be related. I'd love to learn our connection. I look forward to hearing from you!

Or should I lay it right on the line?

I recently learned through my DNA test that my mother cheated on my father and he's not my biological dad. I'm hoping you might be open to sharing your private tree, which could hold a clue to my real father's identity. I'd be forever indebted.

Too honest and putting too much pressure on the guy?

I had to be careful not to scare off someone who didn't want to be responsible for letting skeletons out of a closet.

I never dreamed *I'd* be the skeleton in someone's closet.

However, being my second cousin, it was unlikely that this guy personally knew my father. The more removed, sometimes the more likely people were to assist.

I stared at the empty message box. The person on the receiving end might hold the key to my biological father's identity. That was a lot of pressure on *me* to word the message exactly right so he'd reply!

Needing time to process this new lead and ponder what to say, I closed the message box and clicked on Ethnicity. Simon and I shared English and French backgrounds. I clicked on Shared Matches. Our closest match was a third-to-fourth cousin with no tree. Big help. Yet it was. I could reach out to all the shared matches who could hopefully provide ancestors back to great-grandparents. Even if it meant contacting all their relatives to do so. Then I could compare those surnames to the ones in Simon's tree.

If Simon was willing to share his tree with me.

This would give me something to work on while I was snowbound at the B & B. Along with writing stories in the schoolhouse journal and documenting my family folklore. I was going to be way too busy to lose my sanity and morph into Jack Nicholson's psycho character in *The Shining*.

The first person I wanted to share the DNA news with was Grandma. I'd have to stop by the cemetery on my way to Edmond's. Dad wasn't at the top of my list. It still felt odd discussing it with him. If I ever learned my biological father's identity, I might still be hesitant to share it with Dad. My next thought was to call Finn. Before Biddy? Only because he could relate to what I was feeling.

What *was* I feeling?

My emotions were all over the place!

I hauled Edmond's boxes out to the car. Pinky was in the yard eating breakfast. He slid a curious glance my way, probably wondering why I was packing up my car.

"I'm even going to miss you," I said.

Just when I was making progress overcoming my fear of sheep, I was leaving Ireland. Not like it was forever. Yet leaving Grandma's made it feel that way.

I unloaded a stack of casserole dishes from the car and carried them into Edmond's small kitchen. No curtains and no décor on the bare yellow walls, and merely an electric teakettle and a half-empty whiskey bottle sat on the countertop. A true bachelor's pad. And the bachelor was dressed in the same wrinkled white oxford and blue slacks he'd worn the other day.

"I have more meals if you have room." I opened the fridge door to find two lonely takeaway containers, a carton of eggs, and a few rashers wrapped in plastic.

Edmond peered over my shoulder. "As you can see, there's plenty of room."

I stuck one dish in the fridge, then opened the freezer to stash the rest. A lone tray of ice cubes sat on a shelf. For whiskey, no doubt. I stored the three dishes, swallowing the lump of emotion in my throat. This might be the saddest thing I'd ever seen.

"I'll bring more by later."

"And I'll be sure the dishes make it back to their owners."

Several of the ladies had brought food in glassware labeled with their names.

I'd have to ask Biddy to make Edmond a home-cooked meal once a week. Recalling the time Biddy made French toast and mistook the ground cumin for cinnamon, I decided instead to ask Ita to cook for Edmond. Biddy was no domestic goddess, but neither was I. I'd once made macaroni in the microwave without adding water, and it started a fire.

Edmond and I went into the living room. I unboxed Grandma's computer while he made room for it, relocating stacks of research from the desk to the floor.

He eyed the computer with a sense of apprehension and

dread. "Not much good when it comes to computers. Maggie was a whiz on the yoke. Amazing how much of her research, her life, is in that one black box."

I nodded. "Biddy will give you some training. And when I'm back in April, I can help you run the invite list for the reunion this summer."

Edmond smiled with interest. "A reunion? I'd been hoping to hold one, but it was a big endeavor for just myself."

I told him about the prospective buyers coming to look at the house. "I'm going to ask them about having the annual photo taken in front of the house. We can use Biddy's pub for the event and maybe put a tent up outside."

"A tent would be grand."

"I promise to email often and will send a few postcards from Maine." It would make us both feel good to carry on Grandma's and my postcard tradition.

"I might have my paternal family tree to work on." If I could figure out how to word my message to Simon Reese. I told Edmond about my new DNA match.

"Ah, that's grand, isn't it now? Don't know how that all works, but certainly hope it works out for ye."

"Thanks. Finn and I joked about starting a DNA support group. But that won't be happening now." A sick feeling churned my tummy.

"Sounds like a brilliant idea. Why not give it a go?"

I filled him in on Finn calling off the search for his father and returning to Wexford. I was still upset over Finn insisting that running away, rather than bringing Stella to justice, was the right decision. Yet, I was saddened by the way things had ended. Now more than ever I needed a support group.

For a lot more than just DNA.

I entered McCarthy's pub, where Biddy's dad was stocking the beer cooler behind the empty bar. I slid up on a stool.

"Could be using a pint, could ya?" he asked.

"I look that bad?"

He eyed my swollen lip with concern. "Seen ya looking better."

"I fell at the tractor run."

Thanks to Stella whacking me on the head. Biddy and I'd agreed not to tell anyone about what had happened. If we gave the woman a heads-up, she'd be off to Lanzarote to enjoy an early retirement.

Daniel set a glass of cider ale on the bar.

I couldn't recall ever having drank before noon, yet I took a sip, savoring the sweet apple taste. "Showing my grandma's house to Siobhan and Dylan Farrell this afternoon."

"Ah, fine couple. They'll be grand."

I nodded. "Sounds like it."

"*You* don't be sounding so sure." He closed the cooler and rested his forearms on the bar, giving me his full attention.

"No, I am. They'll be great." I took another drink. "Just a bit down about leaving is all. I had a nice surprise though. Got a second-cousin DNA match."

He smiled. "A promising lead?"

I shrugged. "Best one I've had anyway."

"A bit frustrating I'm sure, especially with your mum being gone, unable to give ya answers."

Yeah, the one person who held the answer to my father's identity had taken it to her grave. I had the right to know my father, as did Finn, even if he claimed he was no longer searching for him. Didn't Biddy's dad have the right to know if he was Finn's father?

"Ever been to Liverpool?" I asked.

Biddy was so going to kill me.

"Still thinking about a holiday, are ya?"

I nodded.

"Been there a few times. For a bachelor's party and to visit a friend. It's grand, especially for Beatles' fans."

"Are you a fan?"

He shrugged. "Would suppose so."

This was getting me nowhere.

"Were you in Liverpool to see a Beatles tribute band on January 8, 1990?"

He laughed. "Ah, I don't believe so. Never seen a Beatles tribute band, and January in Liverpool sounds as brutal as Ireland. Would have been spending my quid on someplace warm. Yet that was back when Ita and I were newly married, so wouldn't have been taking holidays." He quirked a brow. "Why January 1990?"

I filled him in on Finn from the moment he showed me his family photo until he'd returned to Wexford this morning.

He nodded, straightening up from the bar. "I see." Rather than guilt over an affair, his expression was a mix of disappointment and hurt.

"I'm sorry we weren't up front about it when we showed

you the photo. We were certain you couldn't be Finn's father. So asking you would have seemed like we had doubt. I just felt I needed to officially rule you out." A white lie was better than telling him Biddy and I'd both been freaking out over the prospect of him having been Finn's father.

He smiled faintly. "I can say *without* a doubt, I am not Finn's father."

I stifled a relieved sigh. If he'd confessed to being Finn's father, everyone's lives would have changed, including mine. Biddy's dad was my second dad. Well actually, now my third dad.

"But if I were, I'd certainly want to know. And Finn has a right to know."

Despite his fear and frustration, deep down Finn likely still wanted to find his father. For me, curiosity and justice were winning out over fear. I could have died from that blow to the head. People couldn't be allowed to run others off the road and whack them over the head without consequences. If one person got away with it, what was stopping others from committing similar crimes? I couldn't stand by and let crime run rampant in my ancestors' homeland. It could become like the lawless wild west without a fearless Wyatt Earp to enforce justice.

"Please don't tell Biddy I told you all this. She didn't want me saying anything until we'd identified Finn's father. I don't see how I'm ever going to be certain about any of the potential fathers unless I point-blank ask them."

He gave me a sympathetic smile and a bag of comfort food—salt-'n'-vinegar potato chips. "Honesty is usually the best policy."

Not sure Biddy would agree.

Seventeen

I HEADED toward Drumcara to get a shot of Stella's bumper and trick her into giving me back Finn's photo. I passed through a village square where Mickey Molloy was heading out of a hardware store. I waved and veered into a parking spot. He was alone. I had to seize the opportunity to discuss Finn. Asking an older man I barely knew if he'd had an affair seemed a bit disrespectful. However, he and Peter shared the number one spot on my list of potential candidates.

I took a deep breath to calm the nervous fluttering in my chest and headed across the street toward Mickey.

Upon spotting me, he smiled. "Was just thinking 'bout you. After you left the pub the other night, was wishing I'd asked ya for another snap for Brody."

"Ah, sure." I slipped a photo from the envelope in my purse and handed it to him. "Who's Brody?" Why was that name familiar?

"Sorry. I forget you're not from these parts. He's my cousin. A publican in Drumcara."

That's right—George had mentioned his brother Brody owned the bar that first day we'd met.

"His family were the owners of this little fella." He pointed at the dog in the photo. "Charlie, the star of *Charlie to the Rescue*."

From Mickey's and Tommy's warm and loving reactions about Charlie, I'd assumed the dog had been one of their pets.

"Was that a TV show?"

"Aye, but he also starred in movies, one with Maureen O'Hara and another with Barry Fitzgerald. It was shortly after World War Two. He saved the movie studio from bankruptcy. Was a national hero as much as a celebrity. Also starred in loads of commercials and ads for Keegans."

Finn's dad's favorite whiskey!

"Charlie's offspring continued in their father's footsteps. Built up quite the family business."

And quite a family fortune, no doubt.

George might not have recognized the boys in Finn's photo, but he'd certainly have recognized Charlie. He'd never mentioned the dog to me. Had he mentioned him to *Finn*? If my family had a claim to fame like a celebrity dog, I'd certainly be telling people about it. Maybe bragging got old after fifty years.

Mickey's son Mattie approached carrying two cans of paint. Biddy hadn't determined if the cat fur in our pockets had set off Mattie's sneezing fit at the tractor run. Her focus had turned to finding me.

Mattie smiled hello. "Putting in a higher fence. One of the lads got his blue sweater stuck on a post when trying to escape."

Like Biddy getting speared by a post when escaping the cemetery.

Mickey thanked me for the photo and left to paint.

I hopped in my car and continued on to Drumcara. Too bad I didn't have the chance to discuss Finn with Mickey, but I'd certainly be discussing this new bit of info with George. Why hadn't he mentioned that he *had* recognized one of the young fellas in the photo? Charlie.

Was *George* Finn's father?

"I'd like two bags of crisps, a lotto ticket, and the photo you swiped from Finn O'Brien's hospital room."

I smacked a palm against the steering wheel. That wasn't going to work. Maybe Stella would be so riddled with guilt over Finn's accident, and whacking me on the head, that she'd hand over the photo. My plan to sneak a picture of her car's front bumper was dashed when it wasn't parked at her townhouse or the store.

After she found me snooping, she'd likely hidden the car until she could get it in for repairs. Or it was in a shop right now having the evidence buffed out. I'd have to locate the shop and interview the repair guy. I wasn't giving up. I'd find the evidence to prove my Little Red Riding Hood theory to that skeptical garda officer.

I entered O'Sullivan's pub, prepared to confront George. Instead, a tall, ruggedly handsome man with salt-and-pepper hair stood behind the empty bar. His sun-kissed skin had a healthy glow, like he'd just returned from holiday in Spain. Unlike George's typical vintage rock T-shirt, he had on a lightweight sapphire-colored sweater that made his eyes look even bluer. He smiled hello, and a dimple creased his cheek. More so than his brother George, he resembled his cousin Mickey.

And Finn.

Heart racing, I slid up onto a barstool. "I'm surprised George isn't working."

"I just returned from holiday last night, so he decided to be taking the day off. I'm his brother Brody O'Sullivan. New to the area, aren't ya?"

"Mags Murray. I was talking to your cousin Mickey over in Ballycaffey, and he thought you might like a copy of this photo." I slipped the picture from my purse and handed it to him.

His eyes widened; his breath caught in his throat. He brushed a gentle finger over the photo. He glanced at the back, then shook his head, a reminiscent smile curling his lips.

He'd instinctively checked for the phone number despite the photo being a copy. Why else would he have looked at the back? To check for a date? No. It had to be about the phone number.

Brody returned from his stroll down memory lane. "Lovely snap. Will frame it behind the bar." He gestured behind him to the framed vintage whiskey ad with the dog. Charlie. The clue had been right in front of me the entire time. "The locals will appreciate a bit of history. Thanks a mil. Where did ya be getting it?"

From your son.

His reaction proved he was Finn's father.

Yet how many times had I said that?

"From a friend. Mickey mentioned that Charlie saved the movie studio from bankruptcy."

"And my family from poverty. My great-grandfather was killed in the war, leaving my dad's mum with six wee ones at home. Charlie passed on before I was born. However, I was quite attached to his grandson Sammy, who continued in his grandfather's footsteps."

"Did he also have a TV show?"

"Ah, indeed he did. Filmed in Liverpool."

Liverpool?

"When abouts was that?" I maintained a calm tone despite the excitement zipping around inside me.

"Late eighties to early nineties. I traveled back and forth between there and our family home in Galway."

Galway?

My palms started sweating.

"How'd you like living in Liverpool?"

He peered down, once again drawn to the photo. "Made some great memories there."

And a son?

"Was George in the family business as well?"

George not having mentioned Charlie had to have something to do with knowing Finn's identity. When Finn had walked into the pub that day, had George pictured Brody thirty years ago?

"No, he wasn't much for the celebrity lifestyle. I admit it got old after a bit. Made starting a family difficult. When Sammy passed in 1999, I opted for a quieter lifestyle, so I moved here and opened a pub. Always liked visiting the cousins in Ballycaffey. Such a rural, peaceful spot."

Except for an attempted murder...or two.

Had George borrowed Stella's car to follow Finn and run him off the road? Then he'd lied to me about why she'd needed it fixed, trying to make her appear guilty? Why would George have wanted to kill his nephew? Too bad George wasn't here so I could gauge his reaction to the photo and maybe solve the mystery.

A group of men walked in and exchanged greetings with Brody, inquiring on his holiday.

"Would you mind if I take a quick picture of you with the photo? Would be great to add it to the schoolhouse's collection."

"Ah, that'd be grand." He held up the photo. Despite a smile, his eyes reflected a sense of regret, a longing to return to Liverpool in 1990.

Brody couldn't go back in time, but he could go forward. With his son, Finn.

Before leaving Drumcara, I sent Biddy a cryptic text that would pique her curiosity and ensure she was waiting for me when I arrived home. The entire drive there I kept glancing in the rearview mirror for Stella's red car. I was glad when it didn't appear behind me. Yet that meant it was likely in the shop. I pulled into the driveway, where Biddy was talking to a middle-aged man and a young couple. The showing.

"So sorry I'm late," I said, stepping from the car and joining my visitors. I fought the urge to pull Biddy aside, eager to tell her about Brody O'Sullivan.

Rory Lynch smiled, looking much like his brother Ian and nothing like Finn. "No worries. I was just showing

Dylan and Siobhan here the backyard while we were waiting. Can't believe the original stone wall is still intact."

Siobhan nodded. "We wouldn't dream of tearing it down. Or that lovely ash tree."

The lovely ash tree that held my two wishes.

One of which might soon come true.

Should I remove the other wish before selling the house or leave it hidden there with the hope that it might one day come true? And hope that the new owners wouldn't find the slip of paper and the fairies would refuse to grant the wish, no longer a secret.

Biddy smiled. "Ah, that's grand, isn't it now?" She nudged me with her elbow.

I forced a smile when I should have been doing a jig that they'd apparently agreed to my stipulations in the sales agreement.

I escorted them through the mudroom, pointing out the white alarm box by the door. "The security system is on the fritz."

"No worries," Dylan said. "Will have it fixed. This is a safe area. One of the reasons we like it."

I opened the French doors into the living room, where the temperature dropped ten degrees. Siobhan shivered, attempting to rub some warmth into her arms. Had I subconsciously left the peat unlit in the cast-iron stove and kept the curtains drawn to block out the heat from the sun?

"The fuel oil was stolen two years ago. The thief drilled a hole toward the bottom of the tank. Grandma had it plugged, but I wouldn't trust it to hold more than a hundred liters, below the hole." I banged a fist against the radiator, and it kicked in. "Most of the radiators need to be replaced. If you give this one the right touch, it'll put out some heat. You'll also want to have the boiler checked."

"We prefer a fireplace," Siobhan said. "Much cozier. Will be warming up outside soon."

We walked into the conservatory, where water dripped from the ceiling into the kitchen garbage can. "A bit of a leak."

Dylan's gaze traveled from the leaking roof to the fogged windows with broken seals, allowing moisture between the glass panes. "I'm in construction. Plan to replace the structure with a proper, sturdier one."

I gestured out to the woodshed. "Even the shed's rusted padlock needs replacing."

"Ah, that's minor," he said.

Feeling defeated by Dylan's unwavering optimism, I trudged up the spiral staircase, weighted down by an overwhelming sense of sadness and loss. We started in the lavender office.

"Aww, this will be making a lovely nursery." Siobhan placed a hand on her flat abdomen.

We all congratulated the couple on their exciting news.

Dylan smiled proudly. "We're due in June."

My smile faded. "I was going to ask about having the school reunion photo taken here in June, but probably not a good idea with you just bringing the baby home."

"Ah, that's grand," Dylan said. "Many of our relatives attend the reunion, so perfect time for them to meet our new family addition."

This guy's sunny disposition was annoying me.

Siobhan placed a hand on my small desk. "This is the most precious thing ever. Are you selling it with the house?

In a few years, the wee one and I'll be able to work beside each other."

Tears filled my eyes at the thought of leaving behind the desks. I'd always imagined one day my child and I'd sit beside each other, like Grandma and I had for years...

"I can't sell," I blurted out.

Rory, Dylan, and Siobhan looked shell-shocked.

Biddy let out an excited squeal, then gave the couple an apologetic look.

Being a vagabond had been great when I'd had Grandma and her house to come home to. Experiencing new adventures no longer held the same excitement. It was like I'd be wandering aimlessly between jobs with no destination in mind. Since the final destination had always been Ireland.

As it should be.

"I'm so sorry. I thought I was ready to let the house go, but I'm not."

"Ah, right then." Dylan nodded. "Too bad. The place would have been perfect. But we understand." His wife didn't look nearly as forgiving, glaring at me, and Rory looked confused, since I'd just hired him yesterday to sell the place.

The couple left, and I apologized to Rory once again for wasting his time.

"No worries, luv. Was but a few hours of my time spent here, whereas it'll likely be a lifetime for you. If you'd like, I'm sure my dad would be happy to be taking a look at your radiators."

I told him about his father's kind offer.

"And I know plenty of contractors and handymen that would be willing to assist a lovely lass with repairs."

Excluding Dylan Farrell.

He wished me the best and motored off in his blue car.

I stood staring at Grandma's...or rather *my* home. My cute little yellow cottage with a green door and window boxes. I inhaled the comforting scent of peat, the white clouds puffing up from the chimney and into the air.

Rory's comment still played in my head.

It'll likely be a lifetime for you...

It would be. I couldn't imagine ever living anywhere else.

Eighteen

WHEN I WENT INSIDE, Biddy threw her arms around me. I didn't even complain about her crushing my sore shoulder.

"This is totally brill. We're going to be neighbors."

Reality set in, along with panic. "Besides all the repairs, how am I going to afford electricity, fuel, water…"

"No charge for water. Even if they reinstate the water bill, you can hire the bloke in the black hoodie to break your meter."

"If I could afford him."

"Two bottles of cheap whiskey and my friend Imelda's meter was completely banjaxed. You could afford him."

"Maybe I can get another job along with my caretaker one. There can't be more than a few hours of work to do a day without any guests there. I'll use the money from that gig to replace a few radiators. What am I going to do for a job here?"

"Anything. You have a background in almost everything."

"But I have no longevity. Who's going to hire me?"

"My dad's always needing an extra hand at the pub. But

it can be part time because before long you'll be a full-time genealogist. And I'll be keeping an eye on the place. Even better, I could live here, be *your* caretaker. Would love to be getting out of my parents' house for a bit."

What if I returned and Biddy refused to move out, claiming squatter rights? She used a different bath towel daily yet hated doing laundry. She was a morning person. I had little tolerance for perky people before my caffeine fix. Hmm...

Maybe Biddy and I weren't the perfect *couple*. If I'd overlooked our differences in these minor areas, I could certainly overlook flaws in a man. His inability to make me laugh was still a deal breaker.

"Why didn't you question Rory as long as we had him here?"

I perked up. "Because I found Finn's father."

Biddy rolled her eyes. "Again? How many fathers does the fella have now?"

"I'm sure this time." I pulled up Brody's photo on my phone.

"Ah, nice-looking bloke for an older man."

I told her about my conversation with Mickey and Brody.

Biddy's eyes widened. "He had a TV show filmed in Liverpool and was living in Galway?"

"And the dog endorsed Keegans whiskey. But it was the way he looked at the photo, like memories of that night with Finn's mom came flooding back. And he checked the back of it, as if looking for his phone number. He has to be Finn's father."

"Why wouldn't George have told Finn he recognized

Charlie in the photo? I'm sure Finn would have mentioned it if he had. And according to Finn, the man was a great listener that day he was showing the photo around the pub."

"Maybe George realized Charlie, not one of the boys, was Finn's relation, and *George* ran him off the road." I paced across the living room rug.

"But the evidence is on *Stella's* car. Although he could have borrowed it, seeing as they work right across from each other."

"So what's George's motive?" I tapped a finger against my lips. "Something to do with the family estate. Maybe Brody and George would have to split the money with Finn and George didn't want to."

"How would he know Finn was Brody's son?"

"Maybe Brody confided in his brother about his one-night stand in Liverpool and having given the woman the photo." I heaved a sigh and dropped onto the couch. "That's a lot of maybes. How are we going to prove any of it?"

After several moments of silence, Biddy perched on the edge of her chair. "We'll hold a wake."

"A wake? For who?"

"Finn."

"Finn's not dead."

"It'll be a *fake* wake." Biddy squealed with excitement. "A killer always shows up at his victim's funeral, skulking around in the background, making sure the person is dead. Stella went to the hospital to confirm Finn was on his death bed. We'll get everyone together, like on one of those whodunnit movies, and then accuse people. Hard for Stella or George to deny his or her guilt in front of everyone. Ask

George why he didn't tell Brody about Finn having stopped in the pub with the photo."

I twisted my mouth in contemplation. "That seems a bit morbid. There must be another option."

"There isn't. And time is of the essence. Stella or George might already be planning the next attempt on your life."

The massive bump on the back of my head throbbed. I could feel a migraine coming on.

"When George sees the photo—the one you gave Brody —behind the bar, he's going to become even more desperate, knowing you've been there to see his brother. If he's already seen it, he might be on his way over here to take care of you once and for all."

The throbbing in my head grew worse.

"I don't see Stella willingly attending Finn's wake," I said.

"We'll hire her to cater it. If you don't press charges, she'll think you didn't know it was her who knocked you out."

"But I was looking at *her* car."

"She can't know for sure you knew it was her car."

"I can't afford to have another wake catered. For my grandma's I blew through her budget and had to dip into my savings. Besides the fact that I still have casseroles from the last wake. I can just reuse those."

"We can't afford to *not* have it catered. We have to get Stella, George, Brody, and the other possible fathers here somehow. They'll want to verify Finn's dead, and hiring them to cater it shows that you think they're innocent. And no self-respecting Irish person would allow secondhand food to be served at his wake."

My head hurt too much to argue. "Brody could supply the booze. George his famous beef stew. The Molloys could provide traditional Irish music. We'll need all the potential fathers here in case I'm wrong about Brody. Which I'm not."

"Once Tommy Lynch hears there's free whiskey, he'll be here and bring his boys along. Spreading the news of the wake and free booze through our pub will bring in loads of guests. Finn will be quite proud of his wake. Good thing he'll be alive to see how fiercely popular he is."

"Speaking of your pub and getting all the potential fathers together..." I nibbled at my sore lip. "I have to tell you something." I confessed about having confronted her dad on being Finn's father.

Biddy sprang from the couch, a wild look in her eyes. "I cannot believe you did that. You had no right."

"He had the right to know if Finn's his son. And I was able to work it casually into the conversation. It went well."

"That doesn't make it okay." Biddy's gaze softened slightly. "Since we're planning Finn's wake, I'm guessing my dad confirmed he's not his father."

"There's no possibility Finn's his son."

"Or my brother." Biddy plopped onto the couch.

"You're not as happy as I thought you'd be."

She shrugged. "I hated the idea of my father being Finn's dad but kind of fancied the idea of Finn being my brother."

"Well, you certainly can't have one without the other."

She nodded faintly. "I'm still raging that you told my father."

Rather than pointing out the fact that I'd actually never promised not to mention it, I apologized again. The longest Biddy and I'd ever stayed mad at each other was when we were fourteen and I'd told Darragh McNulty that Biddy had the hots for him. She was furious, until he called an hour later and asked her to a movie.

"Hopefully, we can convince Finn we've found his father," I said. "We can't hold his wake without him. And he was adamant about stopping his search. He might be ticked off I didn't listen."

"Once he sees Brody's snap and hears about your meeting with him, he'll be on board with our plan."

"How are we going to convince people he's dead when he's not?"

"We'll lay him out on the far side of the room and somehow block it off, keeping people at a distance so they can't tell he's breathing."

"Maybe he could just hold his breath for an hour." My sarcasm didn't dampen Biddy's enthusiasm.

"Or we could do a limited-time viewing. Like at Murtha's department store when they run a green-light special and you have fifteen minutes to snag the sale item. People will have two minutes to run in and catch a glimpse of Finn."

"Seriously?"

"Okay, we'll figure that all out later."

"Along with how to make Finn appear dead?" Seized with inspiration, I perked up on the couch. "If you use that same makeup on him as you did the day of the tractor run, people will for sure think he's dead."

Biddy typed notes into her cell phone. "We need to write his obituary so we can include the date and time of the wake."

"How are we supposed to write his obit when we know virtually nothing about him?"

"Everyone else around here knows even less about him. Actually, it would be best to have a fake obit to go with the fake wake. And a fake name. Doubt anyone knew his last name or would remember it. Wouldn't want his granny or mum to somehow see the announcement and think he's really dead." Biddy glanced at the time on her phone. "Can probably still get it in the *Examiner's* print and online editions tomorrow."

"Before we go killing off Finn, we'd better make sure he's okay with being dead."

"Just a bit over two hours to Wexford. We'll drive down there to prove just how serious we are." She sprang from the couch. "Best crack on. No time to waste."

I had no clue how we were going to pull this off, but we had to for Finn's sake and my safety. Not like Biddy and I had reputations to protect. If the wake crashed and burned, it'd be par for the course. At least it would give people something to talk about other than my sheep shenanigan.

By the time we reached County Wexford, I was glaring at my phone, fuming. "I can't believe Finn hasn't called or at least texted to see how everything went at the hospital. To see if I ended up with bleeding on the brain or other damage."

Sitting behind the wheel, Biddy let out a frustrated groan. "I'm starting to question the doctor's diagnosis about no brain damage. Jaysus, ya been saying the same thing the entire drive through Wicklow. Sounding like me uncle Seamus after he was kicked in the head by a donkey. His response to everything was 'I was kicked in me head by a donkey.' Auntie Violet would say, 'What ya be wanting for dinner, Seamus?' He'd say, 'I was kicked in me head by a donkey.' 'Then I guess ya don't be wanting donkey burgers,' she'd calmly reply."

"Well, excuse me. I'm feeling a bit emotional. We could be planning my *real* wake right now rather than Finn's *fake* wake, and he couldn't care less how I'm doing. Who was by his side after he was run off the road and lying unconscious in a hospital bed? Me. Who looked like an idiot trying to convince the garda Little Red Riding Hood was out to get him? Me. Who extended her stay in Ireland to help him find his father and get justice—"

"Janey Mac!" Biddy smacked a palm against the steering wheel. "When we get to his house, keep your gob shut and let me do the talking, or he'll never be on board with this."

I dropped back against the seat and mumbled beneath my breath, knowing that drove Biddy bonkers. We were quickly turning into an old married couple. But the more I thought about it, the more upset I became. It was one thing for Finn to have gone back to Wexford before knowing the outcome of my emergency room visit, but then to not even call and check on me? That was downright rude.

Ten minutes later, we pulled up a tree-lined drive. We'd found Finn's address on a "people search" site. Again, why you should occasionally Google yourself to see where you popped up on the web.

An older stately home appeared. A stone wall enclosed the backyard and several outbuildings. Could have been rural Ireland centuries ago if it weren't for the small blue rental car parked in the circular drive.

"Wow. I'd pictured him living in a home like that mod art

monstrosity in Waterford I saw on the tellie," Biddy said. "A white structure with sharp angles jutting out all over. The locals were raging about it upsetting the look of the rural landscape." Biddy's gaze darted to me. "Did you expect him to be living in such a place?"

I shrugged. "I was kicked in me head by a donkey."

Biddy rolled her eyes. She stalked from the car and up the walk. I followed her to the red door with white trim. She rang the doorbell. After several moments, she rang it again.

"Just leave it on the step," Finn yelled from the deep recesses of the house.

Biddy glared at me. "He must be referring to you." She shouted back at the door. "What if she's needing to use the loo?"

Finn answered the door, wearing jeans, a black T-shirt, and a surprised, somewhat confused, look. He raked a hand through his wet hair.

"Sorry for calling in without ringing first," Biddy said.

"Ah, no worries."

He stepped back, and we entered a yellow hallway with two white doors and a white banister and wooden steps leading upstairs. He led us into a sitting room with light honey-colored walls filled with Impressionist landscapes. Biddy and I sat on a green-and-gold upholstered couch facing French doors with a view of a brick patio and green lawn.

Finn's gaze narrowed on me, his brow wrinkled with concern. "How are ya feeling?"

I gave him a tight smile. "Like I was kicked in me head by a donkey."

Biddy tensed next to me.

Finn appeared amused by my odd response, giving me a sympathetic smile. "I'm sure. But ya look grand."

My gaze sharpened. "Yes, well, I could look fine while my brain is bleeding on the inside or suffering from some other horrific head injury. Not that it matters." I peered up at the white crown molding around the chandelier.

"Sorry I didn't ring ya," Finn said. "Was wrecked when I got home and slept all day. Just got up and showered. And realized I don't have your mobile number."

I'd never given him my cell number?

Biddy gloated.

"Sorry." My shoulders relaxed slightly. "I'm just a bit upset that I didn't have the luxury of running away to Wexford. I had to stick around and possibly get whacked on the head again with a tire iron."

Finn's gaze dimmed. "I should have stayed and said a proper goodbye. But if you're that worried, you should leave for the States earlier than planned."

That was his solution?

"I'll be back in the spring for good. What am I supposed to do then? Hide in my house?"

Finn quirked an intrigued brow. "You're keeping your granny's place?"

I nodded.

"That's good. You should."

Why should I?

He held my gaze, and my breathing quickened. There was no mistaking the physical attraction between us, but we both knew this wasn't the right time to act on it. He needed to spend time getting to know his father. While I needed to spend time getting to know myself. If it were meant to be, our paths would cross somewhere down the road. A road in *Ireland* now that I'd be living here. At the moment, I needed to focus on Biddy's and my somewhat morbid idea for uniting Finn with his father and outing Stella, hopefully not George, as the wannabe murderer.

I slipped my phone from my purse and pulled up the photo of Brody standing holding a copy of Finn's photo. I handed it to Finn. He peered at the tall, broad-shouldered man staring back at him with his same bright-blue eyes. A curious glint shown in Finn's eyes.

"That's the same way *he* looked at *your* photo of the four boys and the dog," I said.

"Who is he?"

I told him the story about Brody having lived in Liverpool during the filming of Charlie's show and the dog marketing Keegans whiskey.

Finn nodded, his gaze glued to the photo. "I used to watch reruns of that after school."

"So we'd like you to attend your wake." Biddy perched on the edge of the couch cushion, bubbling with enthusiasm over Finn's supposed death.

Finn looked confused. "*My* wake?"

"It's the quickest way to get this figured out."

His gaze narrowed on Biddy. "You're serious?"

"Do you want Mags to be ending end up in the operating theater?"

"Of course not, but I also don't want to be letting everyone think I'm dead."

"It's not like you'd be lying to your granny or mum. You don't even know the people attending outside of a few brief conversations with George and Stella. Did ya even tell any of them your name?"

He shook his head. "Thought it best not to."

"There ya go. You'd be fibbing to people who don't even know your name. So if ya don't be wanting Mags's death on your conscience, ya should be doing it."

My chest tightened. "I can't continue to live in fear." Not to sound like a total drama queen, but all the talk about my death was freaking me out. I seriously believed Stella wouldn't hesitate to run me off the road if we ever encountered each other outside Drumcara.

Finn peered down at the photo on my cell, then over at me. "You really think he's my father?"

I nodded.

He heaved a sigh, sounding completely overwhelmed. "So what's the plan?"

"Brilliant!" Biddy told him about our plan in a nutshell, since we hadn't yet formulated it. She surged from the couch. "We'll be in touch as soon as we tweak a few details. Must crack on. Long drive back, and I work the early shift."

Finn handed me my phone with a sense of hesitation. Was he reluctant to give up the photo or to perform in his impending wake?

I gave him a reassuring smile. "What's your number? I'll text you a copy."

He gave me his cell number, and I shot him Brody's photo.

"Don't worry. Everything will go just as planned."

Fingers crossed Biddy and I came up with a plan.

Nineteen

BIDDY POWDERED FINN'S NOSE, giving his already white face a more ghostly look. "How's it feel being dead?"

Finn's nose twitched. "Like being a woman." He twisted his mouth around. "Are ya sure that watery clay stuff won't be drying and cracking my face?"

"It's foundation," I said. "My face has never cracked. Now you know what we women go through."

Biddy eyed Finn's white shirt collar. "There's bloody makeup on your collar." Finn had wanted to be laid out in a soccer jersey, but Biddy insisted on a collared shirt, not wanting to have to blend the foundation down to his chest. "No professional makeup artist would allow such a rookie mistake to happen."

"Nobody will get close enough to notice it."

Finn gazed into the mirror, his bruises barely visible beneath the layers of makeup. "To think I could actually have died from head trauma related to the accident and this could really be my wake."

"Nice being alive to enjoy your wake, isn't it now?"

Biddy said. "This is a sort of dry run. If there are things you wished you'd have done differently, you'll have the chance to change it for your real wake. Many would envy such an opportunity."

Finn raised a curious brow. "You have an interesting outlook on life...and death." He peered over at the bed. A new yellow-and-green floral duvet covered the mattress Biddy and I'd flipped that morning. "Would be easier if we'd have done a closed casket. Maybe you could pull the duvet over my head."

Biddy shook her head adamantly. "People need to see you and believe you're dead."

"Biddy and I'll be keeping a close eye on the room. When anyone comes in here, we'll follow them and make sure they respect the boundary and remain a safe distance away." Yellow caution tape served as the barrier, left over from when Biddy's dad had resurfaced their blacktop drive.

Biddy gave Finn's nose one last brush. "Don't forget your name is Finn MaGee."

He wrinkled his brow in disapproval. "Sounds a bit like a leprechaun, doesn't it?"

Biddy nodded. "You never did like your name. You owned a sheep farm in Donegal. No siblings. Your mother, Valerie, lives in Australia. She couldn't make the wake and—"

"My own mother couldn't make the wake?"

Biddy frowned. "Bloody sad, isn't it? And you have no friends is why we're holding the wake for ya. After all, your accident occurred on our roads. We feel a bit responsible. And..."

I swatted Biddy's arm. "He doesn't need to memorize his

fake identity. Not like he's an undercover agent or going into witness protection. He's dead."

"Fine. It was his life. Just thought he might want to know a bit about it."

Finn eased out a nervous sigh.

I placed a comforting hand on his shoulder. "Don't worry—this is going to be the shortest wake in Ireland's history. You won't be lying in bed dead for long."

Biddy shook her head in disapproval. "If anything will give this away as a fake wake, that'll be it. No self-respecting Irish person would hear of having such a short wake."

I rolled my eyes at Biddy and turned to Finn. "Only being two hours will ensure that everyone is here at the same time and not coming and going for days. Like my grandma's wake. We can say we were on a tight budget because you died poor."

"When I was driving a BMW?"

"You lived in your car." Biddy's look turned somber; her eyes watered. "A brutal situation."

I gave Biddy another swat. "Get a grip."

"What if this doesn't work?" Finn said.

I nodded. "It will. We have it all planned out. I'm going to get Brody alone and casually work into the conversation that it was so sad this happened when you'd been in the area looking for your father. That this should have been a joyous first meeting rather than your wake..."

Biddy sniffled, a tear trailing down her cheek.

I shot her a death glare.

She wiped the moisture from her cheek. "A few tears help add a bit of authenticity."

Finn's brow creased with concern. "I hope it's a joyous

occasion. If it is, I have you to thank for not giving up." He peered up at me from the chair. "Besides not having had the right to ask you to quit when you were nearly killed, I should have stayed to help."

I smiled. "No worries. You're here now—that's what matters. And it will be a heartwarming moment."

A sense of renewed hope put a smile on his face, a gleam in his blue eyes.

"I'll finish by mentioning to Brody that your father and mother met in a Liverpool pub. That should be plenty of info for him to realize he's your father."

"We'll immediately tell him you're not really dead, so the poor bloke doesn't have a heart attack or stroke," Biddy said.

"What if he's not my father?"

"Then on to plan B," I said. "If it's not Brody, which I'm ninety-nine percent sure it is, then it's Mickey or Peter Molloy. Once we determine your father, we announce it to the others. Stella will panic that she'd killed a man she'd mistakenly thought was her husband's illegit son and try to sneak out and make a run for the Canary Islands."

"What if it's not Stella?" Finn said.

"It is." I crossed my fingers behind my back, hoping Finn's uncle hadn't tried to kill him. "On the off chance it was George, he'll undoubtedly become overwhelmed with guilt at Brody's breakdown over not having the opportunity to meet his son, and he'll confess."

"No worries," Biddy assured Finn. "We have this planned to a tee. What can possibly go wrong?"

☘ ☘

An hour later, Mickey, Peter, and Mattie Molloy were in the living room warming up their fiddles. Edmond was arranging bowls of nuts on the cocktail table, still smiling over the fact that I'd decided to keep Grandma's house. He'd readily agreed to participate in our charade, if it meant bringing the person who'd almost killed me to justice. He was assisting guests so Biddy and I could keep an eye on people entering Finn's room.

George O'Sullivan exited the kitchen as I was entering. Rather than his usual vintage rock T-shirt, he had on a blue button-up shirt and black slacks. "The stew is in the cooker," he said. "Will be grand for several hours." His blue eyes dimmed. "Still can't believe this happened so suddenly. He'd seemed on the mend at the tractor run. In fine shape and spirit."

The man's grief seemed genuine, not tainted with guilt.

"That's the problem with head injuries. One minute you're fine, the next you're not."

That could have been the case with my head injury. This could have been my wake as well as Finn's. Our *real* wakes. I didn't want to believe George could have done this to either Finn or me. Stella, I believed.

George headed into the living room, leaving Brody and me alone in the kitchen. Dressed in black slacks and a white shirt that showed off his bronzed skin, Brody was lining whiskey bottles up on the counter, along with extra glassware from the pub. Perfect time to kick off Biddy's and my plan.

I took an encouraging yet shaky breath. "Thanks again for providing the alcohol last minute. This was all such a shock."

"No worries, luv. Glad to help out. Wish I'd had the

chance to meet the lad. George said he was an awfully nice fella."

Thankfully, Brody would have the chance to know his son. My eyes watered, imagining their first meeting taking place within the hour. How both of their lives were about to change forever.

"Forgot the extra bottles of Jameson, so making a quick run back to the pub."

Panic dried my eyes. "You can't leave."

"It'll be grand. Won't take more than a half hour."

"We'll be fine with what we have here."

"Promise ya won't even know we're gone." He and George left the house, and moments later a truck roared to life.

Biddy flew into the kitchen. "He can't be leaving. He's the star of the show. Where's he off to?"

I dropped back against the counter. "Getting more whiskey."

"We don't need more bloody drink—we need him here."

"I told him that." I groaned in frustration. "Well, we can't do anything until he returns."

Edmond joined us, appearing a bit frazzled. "Tommy Lynch and his son Ian are here with a few mates from the pub." He lined up seven glasses on the counter.

"A few?" I said. "Go light on the whiskey. It has to last two hours."

I walked into the living room as Stella entered through the French doors, carrying a tray of her famous cupcakes. I suddenly felt underdressed in my basic purple dress and black flats. Penciling in my eyebrow and swiping on mascara was it for makeup. She was wearing a stylish black dress and heels, makeup and coral lipstick, and her blond hair was pulled back in a twist. At least she had the decency to appear like she was in mourning.

"Thanks so much for making those," I said.

"No worries. Hope you enjoy them." She handed me the tray and turned to leave.

"Wait. I need to pay you." And she couldn't leave before George and Brody returned.

"I have a date."

Couldn't she have brought him to the wake?

I zipped into the kitchen and set the cupcake tray on the counter. "Stella's here and about to leave."

Biddy's eyes widened. "Janey Mac! She can't leave until Brody's back. We have to stall her. I'll tell her I have to run home and get money."

"You can't leave me here alone."

Biddy's gaze skittered around the room, searching for a stalling tactic. "I've got it." She slipped a twenty-euro bill and her phone from her back pocket.

I followed Biddy out to the living room, curious how she would detain Stella. Biddy paid her and said, "I was telling my dad about your brilliant cupcakes. He wants to order them for several upcoming events at the pub."

Stella smiled. "That's lovely. Ring me with the dates." She turned to leave, and Biddy grabbed her arm.

"I need to give them to you. They're very soon. Forgot to write them down. I'll ring him now. If you'd like, help yourself to some food and drink."

Stella glanced at her watch and Biddy's hand still grasping her arm. Biddy slowly lowered her hand.

"Suppose I can wait a few minutes." Stella went over to a

cookie tray on the cocktail table, and Edmond swooped in and offered her a drink.

I gave Biddy a thumbs-up, then wiped the sweat from my upper lip. Besides being nervous about our plan going off without a hitch—which it wasn't—the place was like a sauna. Earlier when I'd given the radiator a swift hit, the heat had kicked in full force, and now it wouldn't turn off. I struggled once again with the knob at the base of the unit refusing to budge. I opened the windows, and a cool breeze blew inside.

"I seriously think I'm going to pass out," I told Biddy. "I'm going out to cool down. Be right back."

Standing in the driveway, I peered around for my buddy Pinky and spied a red car parked behind several gray ones down the narrow road. I glanced behind me, making sure Stella wasn't standing there with a tire iron. If she caught me snooping again, I'd likely end up in her trunk this time. Coast clear, I bolted over to her car. I snapped a picture of the damaged bumper still intact. What arrogance...or stupidity to drive to the wake in the car that'd killed Finn. She'd undoubtedly expected to drop the cupcakes and run.

My hands balled into fists at my side, I marched into the house. Stella wasn't in the living room or conservatory, so I poked my head in the kitchen, where Biddy was pouring from the *fourth* bottle of whiskey.

"Have you seen Stella?"

"No. Been in here getting bloody drinks for Tommy Lynch and the lads. Afraid if I don't, they'll just be taking the bottles out to the conservatory with 'em."

I gasped. "Finn!" I flew across the cottage to Grandma's

bedroom as Stella ducked under the caution tape and headed toward Finn. "Stop right there!"

Startled, Stella spun around, unaware of Finn's eyes shooting open.

"What do you think you're doing?" I eyed her hand in her coat pocket. "Planning to shoot him to make sure he's dead?"

Finn squeezed his eyes shut, and his brow furrowed in fear.

"What are you talking about?" Stella said. "I wanted to pay my respects before I leave."

"You're not going anywhere. Slowly remove your hand from your pocket."

Stella's shoulders dropped in defeat. She slipped her hand, along with Finn's photo, from her pocket. "I wanted to return this."

"I knew it. Stay right here while I call the garda."

"I'm returning it. Do you really need to be involving the guards? I feel awful for having taken it, but Sean's affairs embarrassed me enough while he was alive that I wasn't allowing 'em to do so now that he's dead. I shouldn't have nicked the snap from the lad's hospital room, but if Sean was his father, I didn't want everyone to know."

"This isn't just about the photo, and you know it. Yet a murder charge wasn't worth it when Finn isn't even Sean's son."

Stella smiled at the news flash that Finn wasn't her husband's illegitimate son. Her celebration was short lived, and her brow wrinkled in confusion. "Murder charge?"

"You running him off the road. He ultimately died from accident-related injuries."

Her eyes widened. "Are ya mad? I didn't run him off the road. I don't have to stand here and be accused of such a horrible thing."

I flew out into the living room and threw myself in front of the French doors, blocking the woman's escape. "You're not leaving with the evidence."

The happy fiddle tune came to an abrupt halt, and all eyes were on us. Biddy shot me a questioning look. This wasn't part of our plan. I shrugged. What was?

"Fine. Here you go." Stella thrust the photo at me.

I snatched it from her hand, relieved to have it in my possession. "Your car still stays here." I glanced over at Biddy. "Call the garda."

Biddy slipped her phone from her back pocket.

"I didn't drive my car here," Stella said. "It's in the shop. Someone dinged the passenger door. I borrowed a friend's car."

Biddy and I exchanged baffled looks. She lowered her phone.

"If that's not your red car out there with the damaged bumper, then whose is it?" I asked.

Tommy Lynch was strolling through from the conservatory to the kitchen with two empty whiskey glasses. "Ah, that'd be Gretta's. Taking it in to be fixed but decided to call in here first to pay my respects. Don't be telling me someone backed into it again. Guess it'd be good timing since we're having the bumper repaired anyhow."

"That's *Gretta's* red car with the blue paint on the damaged bumper?" I hadn't seen that one coming.

He nodded.

"I'm outta here." Stella pushed past me and out the door

while I stood there dumbstruck.

"When did Gretta supposedly get backed into?" Biddy asked.

"Last Tuesday afternoon when she was running errands."

"Same time as Finn's accident," Biddy said.

"What are ya saying?" Tommy's gaze narrowed. "That Gretta was involved with that lad's accident? With his death? Malarkey. I'll be settling this right now." He called and asked his wife to pick him up because he'd had too much to drink.

If Gretta had held a twenty-year grudge over the daffodils, she'd be taking this one to her grave.

Was she the one who'd locked Biddy and me in the cemetery? Attempting to scare us off after Edmond's and my visit?

Ten minutes later, Gretta stormed into the house, thin lips pressed into a straight line. Before she could blast her husband for being drunk, Tommy filled her in on my accusation that she was responsible for Finn's death.

Rather than once again calling me a little liar, Gretta's stern gaze softened. She slumped onto the couch. "It was an accident."

A collective gasp filled the room.

"I didn't mean to run him off the road. I was following too closely, and he put on the brakes, taking the corner too fast."

"Why were you following him?" Tommy asked.

"It took so long for Maeve to get her life together. I feared that meeting the son she'd put up for adoption years ago and drudging up the past wouldn't be good for her. I was going to plead with him to reconsider searching for her. Offer him money if I had to."

I eyed Gretta. "Hitting me over the head was no accident."

"I didn't think my purse would knock you out cold, merely disorient you long enough so I could get away."

Biddy quirked a brow and mouthed, *Tire iron?*

What did the woman carry in her purse?

"Back to Finn," I said. "He's Brody O'Sullivan's son."

Mickey shot up from his chair, fiddle in hand. "Brody's, you say? Had an affair with Maeve Lynch, did he?"

I heaved a frustrated groan. "Finn has nothing to do with Maeve. We've been trying to find Finn's *father*, who is Brody O'Sullivan."

Everyone's gazes darted to the French doors, where Brody and George stood.

Biddy gave her eyes an exasperated roll. What next? Our well-laid plan was a complete train wreck!

Having apparently heard me reveal his father's identity, Finn walked out from the bedroom. Everyone gasped in shocked horror. Gretta fainted, sliding from the couch onto the floor.

No more saying *what next*.

Finn and Brody locked gazes. The emotional connection and innate bond between the two men was obvious. Just like Finn had always imagined it would be.

I placed the photo in Finn's shaking hand. "You're grand."

He smiled, nodding. He walked over to Brody. "Is this your snap?"

Brody checked the back of the photo. He slowly nodded, peering at Finn through glassy eyes. Without hesitation, he wrapped his son in a tight embrace, just how Finn had imagined it would one day happen.

There wasn't a dry eye in the room. Biddy and I were blubbering over having brought Finn and his father together.

Biddy joined me. "One day that'll be you."

Hopefully, my biological father accepted me, but you never knew. That was the chance you took when searching for the truth. Sometimes you were better off not knowing, which unfortunately you didn't *know* until it was too late.

Regardless, I was sending my paternal second cousin, Simon Reese, a message tonight.

Brody released his hold on Finn and stood back, admiring him. "Jaysus, lad, a spitting image of your father, ya are."

Finn's smile faltered. "Why didn't you return my mum's calls?"

Brody snapped his head back in surprise. "Never got any messages. When I never heard from her, I assumed she regretted our night..." His gaze darted to his brother, George. "*Did* I receive messages? You were home when I was still in Liverpool."

George stared at Brody in silence, his guilt transparent.

"Did I?" Brody demanded.

"You were going to cancel the show at its height because of her, a woman you'd spent one night with. How could you have thought she was the one after only a night together? I figured you were just looking for a reason to cancel. I didn't think you really felt that strongly about her. You were talking nonsense. The show went on to make our family richer than we'd ever dreamed."

"And *you* went on to marry and have a son because you

stayed at home while I lived in hotels and did all the work."

"I'm sorry." George peered over at Finn.

Finn stared at his uncle in disbelief over the man having acted sympathetic and caring about Finn's search for his father when he'd known the truth all along.

"When you walked into the pub that day, I saw Brody. And then when you showed me the snap, I knew you were his son. The phone number on the back confirmed it."

Brody's face reddened. "You can forget about ever seeing another euro from the estate—I'll make sure of it."

George shook his head, regret in his eyes. "I didn't—"

Brody held up a halting hand. "Just leave."

"I'm sorry," George said to both men and slinked out.

"I'm sorry too," Finn told Brody. "I always feared that finding my father might break up a family."

"By finding me you've brought *our* family together."

Biddy hooked her arm through mine. "See. Everything went exactly as planned."

"As *who'd* planned?" I peered over at Tommy helping Gretta onto the couch after her fainting spell.

"Yeah. Guess we hadn't seen that one coming. But we were right about Stella having taken the snap and Brody being Finn's father. Two out of three isn't bad."

Not with our track record.

I stood by the ash tree in the backyard, peering at the house lit up inside, the chimney puffing white peat-scented clouds into the evening sky. *My* house. And maybe Biddy's. We'd agreed she could live here and watch over the place until I returned from my caretaker gig in April. I still wasn't sold on us being roomies. I didn't want living together to jeopardize our friendship.

I had three months to make a decision.

Biddy's first task as caretaker would be to arrange for more peat and wood to be delivered. Thanks to the rogue radiator not shutting off, the fuel had run out. The paycheck from my caretaker position would go for home repairs. I was a bit nervous over where my checks would come from after April. Even though I was used to not knowing what state my next job would be in, I'd never had the financial responsibility of owning a home.

Finn's mom was flying in from the US the next day to meet with Finn and Brody. When Finn had called and told her about finding his father, and how George hadn't relayed her messages, she'd been happier than he'd expected. It seemed her lack of encouragement and enthusiasm over her son's search for his father had been a self-preservation tactic. All those years she'd tried to suppress her feelings for a man she believed hadn't shared them.

I removed the pink slip of paper from behind the fairy door. My one wish had come true. To find Finn's father. I tucked a green slip into the hiding space, alongside the yellow one with a wish still waiting to be granted.

When Grandma and I'd put in the fairy door, she'd blessed it with an old Irish saying: "May you get all your wishes but one so you always have something to strive for."

In Grandma's memory, I promised to always have at least two wishes waiting for the fairies to work their magic.

And to never give up hope that the wish on the yellow paper would one day come true.

A Mags and Biddy Genealogy Mystery
Book Two

USA Today Bestselling Author
Eliza Watson

Genealogy
Tips & Quips

Genealogy Tips & Quips
Learn About Genealogy Research

Genealogy Research Tips

I wrote the following article about family photos for my nonfiction book *Genealogy Tips & Quips*. In 2018, I began writing a genealogy column for my monthly author newsletter about my personal research experiences. I was writing articles faster than I was publishing newsletters, so I decided to compile them into a book. *Genealogy Tips & Quips* includes fifty newsletter articles and two extensive case studies—one about how a paternal DNA test revealed my family's royal lineage and my quest to uncover family secrets.

Family History Photos
PICTURE YOUR FAMILY'S HISTORY

I've been known to shed a tear when walking into an antique store or consignment shop and seeing boxes of old photos for sale. How sad that nobody in a family wanted their ancestors' photos, even if their identities were unknown. Yet lack of interest isn't always why photos end up in shops, or even worse, garbage dumpsters. Years ago, my dad's cousin offered him a huge stash of old family photos. When my dad went to pick them up, his cousin was in a surly mood and refused to give him the photos. After his cousin passed away, my dad received a phone call from a lady in his hometown—three hours away—who'd bought his cousin's dresser filled with family photos. Luckily for us, someone who knew my dad's family had purchased the dresser.

My mom and I will spend hours looking through boxes of family photos. A few years ago, I came across a black-and-white one of my great-grandparents Dennis Flannery and Erma Hansen dressed in their finest outfits. The name and address of a Chicago photographer was embossed on the lower corner. Why had the couple traveled several hundred miles from their rural Wisconsin farm to Chicago for a photo shoot? My question was answered when a few minutes later I found a postcard of Chicago's Michigan Avenue, which Erma had sent to her mother. The card's postmark enabled me to date the couple's photo almost to the hour it was taken on November 17, 1916. The couple had been married November 15, 1916, so they were obviously on their honeymoon.

In the card, Erma mentioned that Mrs. Kenney was taking them to have their "mugs shot" later that afternoon before going downtown Chicago for dinner. I knew from research that Mrs. Kenney was formerly Mary Flannery, who in 1910 had lived just a few blocks from the photographer located at 220 Cicero Avenue. Between the postcard, photo, and census, I was able to piece together an interesting story about the couple's honeymoon. I plan to frame the photo and postcard, along with the story. And to think prior to being a genealogist I would get upset when a photographer "ruined" a photo with his marketing information on the front.

An Ancestry.com hint for my Flannery family tree clicked through to what became my only photo of my ancestors James and Mary Flannery, who'd emigrated from Castlebar, County Mayo, Ireland. As if that wasn't a huge enough find, the photo also revealed a clue—the photography studio's name and location in Eldora, Iowa. Traveling over a hundred miles from their home in southcentral Wisconsin was quite a distance to have their picture taken. I haven't found evidence that the photographer was a relation they might have been visiting. I Googled the studio and learned that it had operated from the 1860s to the 1880s. Based on the couple's appearance, I estimated the photo was taken in the 1880s. (Knowing a photography studio's name and location is a great way to date a photo.) In the 1880 census, I'd been unable to locate the Flannery family. Was that because they'd possibly moved to Eldora, Iowa? I haven't yet located them in that area, but I'll keep looking. Old photos can provide great clues.

When I shared family photos with our Daly relatives in Ireland, they pointed out that my grandma had the Daly chin and nose as did I. After seeing photos of their grandmother, I totally agreed. I belong to a DNA online group where numerous adoptees who've connected with biological family members post pictures of their newfound relations. The resemblance is often amazing.

Photos offer a peek into your ancestors' everyday lives. Maybe there's a dog in every one of your grandpa's photos confirming he was a dog lover just like you. In almost all the early photos of my mom and her siblings, she is holding their hands or has someone sitting in her lap. As the eldest child, she was a caregiver from a young age. When I was young, my grandma Watson was in her sixties, and I remember her wearing handsewn dresses. Photos from her single life in Milwaukee show she'd been quite the fashion diva. She always wrote an outfit's color and fabric on the back of a black-and-white photo. Same as my grandma, I'd been a total clotheshorse in high school. Years ago, when my husband and I left a seafood restaurant set in a residential area of Milwaukee, I spied a house across the street that I'd seen in many of my grandma's photos. It still had the same shingle siding. The street sign confirmed it was indeed where my grandma had lived.

One picture can literally lead to a thousand words. My grandma Watson gave me a photo of her and a group of girls posing in a city park. They were her coworkers when she lived in Milwaukee before being married and moving back to her small hometown. She shared stories about them going dancing at a place called the Lonely Hearts Club where the men couldn't refuse a lady's dance request. Once the club's owner was married, he renamed it the Friendship Club. What a great story.

My grandma Watson always had a black-and-white photo on her dresser of herself in her twenties, wearing a chiffon dress and cloche hat, holding a parasol. Again, fashion diva. When I mentioned how much I loved the photo, she told me the story behind it. She had tagged along with her older sister on the train to a nearby town for a photo shoot. The photographer had asked to take my grandma's photo, even though she told him she had no money to purchase pictures. A few weeks later, she received the proof in the mail. It turned out my favorite photo of my grandma is actually a *proof*. It is framed and sitting on a shelf in my office.

*Dennis and Erma Flannery's honeymoon photo in
Chicago, Illinois, 1916.*

The fashionable Grandma Zelda Watson, circa 1927.

Author's Note

Thank you so much for reading *How to Fake an Irish Wake*. If you enjoyed Mags and Biddy's adventures, I would greatly appreciate you taking the time to leave a review. Reviews encourage potential readers to give my stories a try, and I would love to hear your thoughts. My monthly newsletter features genealogy research advice, my latest news, and frequent giveaways! You can subscribe to my newsletter at www.elizawatson.com.

Thanks a mil!

About Eliza Watson

When Eliza isn't traveling for her job as an event planner, or tracing her ancestry roots through Ireland, she is at home in Wisconsin working on her next novel. She enjoys bouncing ideas off her husband, Mark, and her cats, Frankie and Sammy.

Connect with Eliza Online

www.elizawatson.com
www.facebook.com/ElizaWatsonAuthor
www.instagram.com/elizawatsonauthor

9 781950 786046